Sharpe Cookie: Two Sides to Every Coin

Maycroft Mysteries, Volume 6

Lisa B. Thomas

Published by Lisa B. Thomas, 2019.

Copyright

SHARPE COOKIE

Copyright © 2017 Lisa B. Thomas

Cozy Stuff and Such, LLC

Chapter 1

SOME OLD HABITS die hard, and as it turned out, this was one of them.

Estelle had insisted that Gary and Deena ride with her and Russell in the old Bentley she had kept around after her parents died. It was pretentious, of course, but Deena didn't want to say anything to upset Estelle.

Her sister-in-law had had a hard time sorting through her parents' old treasures, trying to decide what to keep and what to sell off for charity. Deena figured they might as well humor Estelle if she indeed wanted to show up to the auction in her Cinderella -coach.

Estelle's parents had been big fish in Maycroft's little pond. Her mother was known as the Grand Dame of Maycroft. Estelle's life had turned upside down the previous spring when her mother was murdered. Since then, though, Estelle had blossomed. Still, she had lived most of her adult life caring for her mother, so getting rid of many of the family heirlooms was emotionally wrenching.

Leonard Dietz wore his full chauffeur's uniform for the special occasion. It had been a long time since Estelle had called upon him to drive her. Deena hadn't seen him since shortly after Estelle's mother died. At nearly eighty years old, Leonard appeared a little more wrinkled, a little more gray, and a lot more stooped over than Deena remembered.

She wondered if he still even had a driver's license. Regardless, the community center where the estate auction wasn't that far away. Surely, they could make it there and back without incident.

"I'm going to feel ridiculous getting out of that thing," Russell whispered to Deena as they waited for Estelle out on the front porch of his house. He pulled at the knot on his necktie. Deena's brother still hadn't gotten used to the trappings of wealth he had obtained when he married Estelle the previous spring.

"Why are you telling *me*? Why didn't you say something to Estelle?" Deena asked.

"I did, believe me. But she said this is what her mother would have wanted. Who am I to argue?"

Estelle was right. Carolyn Fitzhugh would have wanted her daughter wearing a long gown, pearls, and a tiara just to remind the small town of Maycroft that the Fitzhugh name was still royalty around here.

Luckily, Estelle appeared on the porch wearing a smart-looking tailored jacket and skirt, more in the style of Jackie O than Princess Di. Ever since she married Russell, Estelle had metamorphosed from a drab, ugly duckling into a beautiful swan. Well, "beautiful" may be a bit strong, but she certainly was attractive. Gone were the unruly gray locks replaced by a trim stylish cut, complete with highlights and lowlights that perfectly accentuated her narrow face.

Deena pictured her own hair, wondering if it was time to stop fighting the gray roots and go lighter.

Mr. Dietz opened the car door. Russell walked a few steps down off the front porch and then looked back at Estelle, who stood still as a statue. Luckily, he realized what he had done and had the good sense to go back for his wife. He crooked his arm and escorted her to the car, depositing her in the back seat. He looked at Gary, apparently sharing some silent bro-code telepathy.

"I got this," Gary said and offered Deena his arm. "Shall we, my lady?"

"Shhh," Deena said. "She'll hear you." He escorted her to the car and deposited her on the opposite side. She scooted over next to Estelle to make room for him. Russell had already taken his seat in the front.

The short ride was pleasant enough. Gary and Russell talked football, while Estelle told Deena what she planned to do with the items she chose to keep instead of sell.

Estelle fiddled with the handle of her sequined purse. "I guess I should hang those large family oil paintings in the ballroom instead of keeping them stored, but they're just so creepy. Mother's eyes seem to follow me wherever I go. And Father, he looks so different than I remember."

Deena pictured the large wedding photo of Gary and her that used to hang in their living room. At some point, it just didn't look right. They weren't those young lovebirds anymore. "I can relate. Our wedding portrait is gathering dust in the attic." She turned toward Gary. "Hey, do you think your mother would like our wedding portrait in her house? Then she could have you almost life-sized."

"I'll ask her." Gary, normally sharp as a tack, didn't catch the sarcasm.

"You guys are like us," Estelle said. "With no children to pass your family heirlooms on to, it's hard to know what to do with them."

"I wouldn't call our picture an 'heirloom' exactly, but I know what you mean."

Estelle pulled out a compact to check her face. She wore the high-end department store brand now instead of the kind she used to buy at the drugstore. "Besides, we're not getting any younger."

"*We're* not," Deena said, "but *you* are. I swear you look at least ten years younger than when I first met you last year."

Estelle smiled. "That's all because of your brother."

It was true. Once Estelle was out from under her mother's thumb, she had blossomed. She wore her sixty-three years of life better than a lot of women Deena knew.

Estelle snapped the compact shut. "Isn't your sixtieth birthday coming up? We should have a party."

"I agree," Gary said. "But Deena won't hear of it."

"You bet I won't. I plan to stay in bed all day and not get up until it passes."

"Oh, fiddle-faddle," Estelle said. "You should be happy you're still alive and kicking. At least let me take you for a spa day. We could go to one of those places in the Hill Country where you drink wine all day and get a proper pampering."

"That does sound good, but it will depend on the day of the week. I'm a working gal now, you know."

"Oh, that's right. I keep forgetting you took over at the thrift store for Sandra. How's baby Sylvia doing?"

Deena cringed. She still hadn't gotten over the fact that her best friend named her only child the same name as her busy-body mother-in-law. "She's perfect. Just beautiful. Oh, and by the way, Sandra asked me to thank you for designating the animal shelter as one of the charities you are donating the auction money to. That's where the thrift store profits go, you know."

"I'm glad to do it. You know I love cats, and Russell couldn't live without that big dumb dog."

"Hey," Russell said, looking over his shoulder from the front seat, "Maggie isn't dumb."

"Then why does she keep eating out of Clover's bowl?"

"Look, we're here," Deena interrupted, not wanting to start a Sinclair family feud.

Estelle had told Deena that when she contacted the Auction Barn to sell off some of her parents' possessions, the owner, Jeb Johnson, knew his small building would never hold the kind of crowd the event would attract. Not wanting Estelle to move the sale up to Dallas, he contracted with the Maycroft Community Center to hold the auction. He had also advertised the heck out of it.

Good thing, too. People called from far and wide to get details, and the town's handful of hotels filled up fast. Not only that, many of the locals planned to be there just to see the vast treasures the infamous Fitzhughs generally kept behind closed doors in their large Victorian mansion. Most people in town referred to it as the "Fitzhugh Estate."

"Wow! What a crowd," Russell said as they rolled up to the front door.

Patsy Johnson, wearing her signature turquoise rodeo outfit, came up to the car window. When she spoke, the words practically bubbled out of her mouth. "Welcome! Let me help you out of the car."

"I'll get that," Leonard called out in his gravelly voice.

It was the closest thing to the Academy Awards red carpet Deena had ever seen in Maycroft. A photographer from the newspaper stood outside the door snapping pictures. People stopped and stared. Estelle even waved to onlookers as though they were fans.

As Gary and Deena trailed behind, she could hear Patsy telling Leonard that she had reserved him a special parking spot right by the back door so they would be able to get out quickly after the event. They were really giving Estelle the VIP treatment.

Patsy caught up to them and led the group through the crowd to a spot on the side of the makeshift stage where the auctioneer's podium stood. It felt awkward to sit on the side where everyone could stare at them. Deena was surprised they hadn't constructed a balcony for them to sit in as though they had box seats at the opera. It felt strange, like sitting in the family section of a funeral, but without all the sympathy.

One of those red velvet ropes, like the kind they have to direct lines at the movie theater, blocked off their row of seats, presumably to keep the riffraff from stepping on their toes.

People milled around getting a last minute look at the items to be auctioned off. The entire left side of the large hall was filled with furniture and folding tables covered with lamps, statues, pottery, dishes, and every kind of objet d' art imaginable. It was a collector's paradise.

"Yoo-hoo!"

Deena recognized that voice. She looked around to see Penelope Burrows from the Bluebonnet Club waving at them. She had on her violet, feathered church hat. No doubt the Styrofoam cup in her hand had been spiked with whiskey. Hard to believe that someone who drank like Penelope did could still be going strong well into her seventies. There were several other club members sitting by her, popping up from their seats to wave in their direction. Estelle and Deena both waved back, while Russell and Gary pretended not to notice. Several other people Deena knew walked by to greet them as well. One of her former students asked Estelle to take a selfie with her.

Deena checked the clock. "Time to get this shindig started," she said to Gary, who was making notes in the auction brochure. Actually, the brochure consisted of a stack of white copy paper stapled together showing black-and-white photos of the items to be auctioned off. Still, compared to the Auction Barn's usual Saturday night fare, it was big time.

"What are you doing?" Deena asked Gary, who busily scribbled on the sheets of paper.

"I'm estimating a price that I think each item will go for. It's like a game show. I want to see how close I come to the hammer prices."

Deena shook her head. *Once an accountant, always an accountant.* By the end of the night, he'd know to the penny exactly how much money Estelle's auction would raise for charity, figuring in Jeb's commission, the selling price, and the ten percent buyer's premium.

If Deena hadn't been accompanying the guest of honor, she might have been bidding on some of the items herself. Occasionally, she was able to drag Gary with her to an auction or a flea market so she could buy things to sell at her antique booth. Usually, she just went alone, leaving him home to watch some "super important" sporting event. However, he drew the line at garage sales. He hated looking through other people's castaways.

If you think about it though, an auction wasn't much different. You were still buying someone else's used stuff. The only real difference was that customers at a high-end auction like this one were looking to buy rare art and Persian rugs instead of old tube socks and headless Barbie dolls.

Deena looked around trying to spot the out-of-towners, the high rollers who had come in to sweep up some rarities from the small-town hicks. Good thing she didn't have a bidding number. She could get very competitive when it came to auctions.

The gavel cracked, calling the crowd to attention. Jeb's microphone squealed at a pitch high enough to rival the Met's top soprano. He adjusted his headphones and welcomed them all. "As you know, all the proceeds from today's auction—minus my commission, of course—will go to local charities."

Polite applause followed.

"And now I'd like to ask Ms. Estelle Fitzhugh to stand."

Estelle rose and the crowd erupted. Patsy rushed up and presented her with a bouquet of red roses as though she'd just won a beauty pageant.

"It's Estelle Fitzhugh *Sinclair*," Russell said, emphasizing her new married name, but no one heard.

Jeb waited for the applause to die down. "Helping me out tonight is my lovely wife, Patsy. Take a bow."

Patsy twirled her cowgirl skirt. She caught the toe of her pointy white boot on a folding chair and nearly took a tumble.

"Err...and my son Leroy and his crew. As you know, Leroy has a moving company and is available to help you with all your transportation needs."

At last, Jeb got on with it. The first item was an English silver tea service. When the hammer came down, it sold for twenty-two hundred dollars.

Things were clipping along. The auction was well into the second hour, and Deena, of course, got hungry. The choir group from the high school was selling refreshments in the back of the hall. She asked Gary if he wanted anything, knowing it would mess up his calculations if he missed any of the action. He declined. Russell went with her to the refreshment area.

She noticed a small group of men who appeared to be arguing near the far back corner. She recognized one of them as Marty Fisk, Maycroft's newly-elected mayor and owner of the Lucky Strike Pawn Shop. Deena, being nosy, debated walking over to see what all the fuss was about. But one of the men's wives dragged him off by the arm and the others went their separate ways. Deena assumed they were arguing over politics since the election had been just a few weeks earlier.

When they got to the front of the refreshment line, she eyed the selections. "Do you think it would be too tacky to buy popcorn? It's not a ballgame after all."

"No. And I wish they were selling beer," Russell whispered.

Deena's brother had not inherited her social gene. He preferred small gatherings and a television to keep him entertained.

"Yeah, that's just what you need at an auction—a bunch of people getting drunk and bidding on pricey antiques." Deena placed her order for soda and a peanut butter cookie and waited for Russell. "So, have you gotten used to being rich yet?"

Russell picked up a stack of napkins. "It's really not much different from before. I still help out Cliff at the repair shop a couple of days a week. It keeps me humble." He gave her a wink. "Biggest difference is that there are rooms I'm not allowed to go into at Estelle's house because of my dirty boots."

"Still calling it 'Estelle's house,' I see."

"Yeah. That'll probably never change." He squirted ketchup on his hot dog, and they made their way back to their seats.

As soon as they sat down, Estelle tugged at Russell's sleeve. "Something happened," she whispered. "While you were gone, they auctioned off my great-grandfather's Civil War diaries. I had put those in the stack of stuff to keep. How do you suppose that happened?"

"I don't know," Russell said, unwrapping his hot dog. "Maybe you put them in the wrong pile."

Estelle shot him a look that clearly said she didn't like his answer.

"Sold! To buyer ninety-five." Jeb banged the gavel, and the auction workers carried off a velvet settee that used to sit in the parlor that was now Russell's man cave. "Next up we have lot number twenty-two. It's an authentic Tiffany lamp. Quite a beauty, ain't she! Who'll start us off at a thousand dollars?"

Estelle grabbed Russell's arm, nearly knocking the hot dog out of his hand. "It's happening again!" This time, she spoke louder. "I'm positive I set that lamp aside to keep!"

Russell wadded up the hot dog wrapper and picked up his Dr Pepper. "Are you sure? You've got lots of lamps that look just like that."

"Uhh," she grumbled. "I'm sure of it."

"Maybe you walk to the back and tell Patsy you want to keep those things."

"And look like an Indian giver? Not to mention how word will spread through town about me taking money away from charities."

"Have you looked at the auction catalog?" Gary asked. He handed her Deena's copy. "You can see everything that's included in the auction."

Grabbing the papers, Estelle jumped as the gavel came crashing down and Jeb announced the selling price of fourteen-thousand dollars for the lamp. She flipped wildly through the pages, not seeming to focus.

Jeb pointed to a large framed canvas that one of the guys set on an easel. "Next up, we have this beautiful oil painting of Captain Charles S. Fitzhugh, dated 1867. Who'll start us out—"

"No!" Estelle screamed and leaped out of her chair. She ran up to the front of the hall and grabbed the painting. The guy standing next to it tried to wrestle it away. Estelle kicked him in the shin and ran carrying the painting toward the side door.

"You get him, sister!" someone shouted. Penelope Burrows stood waving her fist.

The crowd erupted in a combination of laughter and gasps.

Another man chased Estelle out the door.

Then a shrill scream came from outside. It was not the kind you normally hear. It was bone-chilling.

Russell jumped up and ran for the door. Gary and Deena sat frozen, not really knowing what to do. It seemed as though all eyes turned to them at once.

The man who had chased Estelle reappeared. "Call 9-1-1! There's been an accident!"

Deena's heart skipped a beat. She pictured Estelle lying on the pavement, blood pooling under her head, the old painting crumpled by her side. Had she run into the street and been mowed down by a car?

Gary grabbed her arm and pulled her toward the exit. Others stood up but let them pass before following them outside.

Relief washed over Deena as she spotted Russell and Estelle standing next to the Bentley. She let out her breath and almost smiled. But where was the accident?

Then she saw a uniformed security guard running toward Estelle and the Bentley. Although the car was parallel parked, Deena could tell the driver's door was open.

Then it hit her. Where was Leonard Dietz? Gary rushed up to Estelle as Deena headed around the front of the car. The guard held out his arms. "Stay back, ma'am."

He nudged her backward but not before she got a glimpse of Leonard. He lay on the ground with a pool of blood under his head. It was just how she had pictured Estelle. The painting was even on the ground next to him.

To Deena, he looked dead.

Chapter 2

WHAT HAD HAPPENED? He was slumped over next to the curb, so he couldn't possibly have been hit by a car. Had he fallen and cracked open his head?

Sirens pierced the night air. A crowd of onlookers lined up on the side of the building. Patsy Johnson tried to coax everyone back inside. "Let's go, folks. Let the police do their job."

Deena rushed over to Estelle. "What happened?"

"I—I don't know." Tears rolled down her cheeks and dripped on her blazer. "I came outside and ran around the side of the car. Leonard was just lying there." She put her hands over her face. "Did you see him? Is he alive?"

Deena glanced at Russell. "I don't know. Let's wait and see."

Two police cars and an ambulance rolled into the parking lot. One of the officers asked everyone to move closer to the building so they wouldn't be in the way. The paramedics rushed to Leonard's side. The officers moved deliberately. Several of them huddled together while another talked on his radio. It wasn't long until the flurry of activity seemed to slow down.

An officer approached Estelle. He seemed to walk in slow motion. Deena recognized him as Officer Hitchcock. Maybe he was as hesitant to talk to them as they were to hear what he had to say.

"Ms. Fitzhugh?"

"Yes."

"Is that your car?"

"Yes."

"And was that man your driver?"

Deena caught the way the officer referred to Leonard in past tense.

Estelle nodded.

"I'm afraid he didn't make it."

Estelle sobbed and buried her face in Russell's shoulder.

Deena flashed back to the day Carolyn, Estelle's mother, died and Russell was there to comfort her. It seemed like ages ago.

The officer turned to Gary and Deena. "I'm going to need a statement from her since she was the first one on the scene."

Deena nodded. It was going to be a long night.

Officer Linndorf came up to Hitchcock and held out his hand. "Check this out. I picked it up off the ground next to the car."

In his large, gloved hand was a shiny, gold object. Deena leaned in closer and saw a coin.

Hitchcock pulled out a handkerchief and took the coin from Linndorf. "Are there any more?"

"I'll check." He turned on his flashlight and leaned down next to the Bentley. "Here's a couple more." He brought them back and handed them to Hitchcock.

Right then, Jeb Johnson appeared out of the side door of the building. "Um, Miss Estelle, the police have advised us to cancel the rest of the auction. We'll have to reschedule it for another time."

Hitchcock shined his flashlight on the handkerchief. "Say, Mr. Johnson, have you ever seen coins like these?"

Jeb slid his reading glasses down from the top of his head to his nose. "I'm no expert, but those look to be coins from the auction."

Estelle gasped. "My father's coin collection?"

"Let me get one of the fellows from inside who can tell us for sure." Jeb disappeared back into the building.

People flooded into the parking lot, trying to get a glimpse of the accident scene. Another few police vehicles arrived, and several officers directed traffic away from the area.

Jeb came back out followed by the mayor. "Here, take a look at these, Marty. Are these from the collection?"

Fisk looked closely at the coins, being careful not to touch them. He bolted upright. "You bet they are. These are rare coins. I had been looking at them earlier."

As though spectators at a tennis match, they all turned simultaneously to Jeb as though he would have an explanation.

Luckily for him, one of the auction workers walked up. "Hey boss, I need to talk to you."

Jeb held up his hand to indicate that he needed a minute.

"Are you okay?" Deena asked Estelle. Her color was better, but she was still shaking.

She nodded. "Poor Leonard. I think I knew he was dead the minute I saw him. I was just hoping..."

"I know. Me too."

Deena wanted to go over and ask the paramedics what they thought happened. She could only imagine how the scene looked to the police. They would hear how Estelle ran out of the building with the giant painting and then found Leonard lying next to the curb with his head smashed. Would they think Estelle hit him and knocked him down? Surely not.

Unless it was an accident, and she just wasn't telling anyone. Deena shook off the thought.

Jeb returned, his face a ghostly white. "I'm sorry to say this, but I just got word that your father's coin collection is missing."

"Missing?" Estelle looked wide-eyed and turned to the officer.

Hitchcock folded the handkerchief carefully around the coins. He handed them to Linndorf, who hurried to his squad car.

Hitchcock pressed the button on his shoulder radio. "Listen up, everyone. This is no longer an accident scene. We need the special investigations unit dispatched immediately. This is now a crime scene and should be treated as such."

Chapter 3

MAYCROFT WAS A SMALL town with a population of about eight thousand and change. People generally knew their neighbors and had at least a "nod-and-a-howdy" relationship with most people in town. Much of the town's activity centered around the high school, especially during football season. The supermarket, church, and local eateries were common gathering places.

But Maycroft was not that much different from the big cities. They had crime, corruption, and their share of all the more unsavory parts of community living. There's really no such thing as random violence. You look deep enough, and you'll find a cause, whether it's a turf war or road rage. So far, Maycroft had avoided any terrorist attacks, and the few gangs that had tried to form got quickly thwarted by observant teachers and parents.

One year, some teenagers started wearing bandanas to school as though their teachers wouldn't know what they were for. All the kids got sentenced to cafeteria clean-up duty and that was the end of that.

When it came to homicides, though, they had their fair share. As long as there are people on this earth, you'll see crimes of passion, greed, and revenge.

So what happened to Leonard Dietz? He was not likely the victim of a jilted lover. Deena couldn't imagine him involved in a drug deal gone bad. So what happened?

Cue Detective Guttman.

The police had moved Deena and company inside the community center to wait for Estelle to be questioned. One of the auction workers who hadn't been outside to see the commotion had volunteered to run Gary back to the house so he could get his car. Obviously, the Bentley wasn't going anywhere anytime soon.

Before long, Detective Linus Guttman entered the hall, hands in pockets, looking as if he'd prefer to be anywhere else on that fine November evening.

"You've got to be kidding," he said when he saw Deena. "Not you again."

"I could say the same thing about you. Are you the only homicide cop in Maycroft?" She knew that he was, but she wanted to get in a jab. "I believe you have already met my brother, Russell Sinclair, and this is his wife, Estelle Fitzhugh Sinclair." She emphasized the Sinclair part for Russell's sake.

"Nice to meet you." Detective Guttman didn't offer his hand to shake until Deena gave him the stink-eye. He grimaced, then obliged. It had become a personal mission of hers to teach that Yankee cop some Southern manners.

"So, tell me exactly what happened," he said. "Who wants to start?"

Deena gave him the background info leading up to Estelle finding Leonard Dietz. She left out the part about the tussle over the painting and Estelle kicking the poor auction worker.

Guttman asked Estelle the obvious questions, and she gave the same answers she had already given the other officer. Guttman didn't take any notes. He may have already been briefed on what had gone down. When Estelle finished, he asked her specifically about the coins.

"My father had a large coin collection. I think he had inherited some of the coins from his father. He acquired others over his lifetime. He had some he liked to display and others he just kept loose in a case. Those loose coins were the ones I donated to the auction. The others are at home in a safe." She slapped her hand over her mouth. "Oops. Maybe I shouldn't have told you that."

"I'm a cop. You can trust me."

Deena remembered when Guttman first arrived in Maycroft and she wasn't sure of his integrity. Since then, she'd grown to trust and respect him as an honest officer of the law.

"So these coins," he continued, "were some of them the same ones found outside in the parking lot?"

"According to Mayor Fisk, they were," Estelle said. "I don't really know much about coins myself."

"You said the coins were in a case. What did it look like?"

"It was one of those metal protective ones like photographers carry equipment in." She used her hands to indicate the approximate size. "It was about the size of a briefcase."

Deena picked up one of the catalogs off a chair. "Here's a picture of it."

Guttman studied the picture a minute then put the catalog in his pocket. "Just for the record, did any of you see who took the coin case or have any idea of who did?"

They all shook their heads.

"Do you think Mr. Dietz might have taken it?"

Estelle puffed out her chest. "Leonard? Absolutely not!"

Deena addressed the elephant in the room. "Obviously, you think whoever stole the coins also killed Leonard Dietz. Is that right?"

"It's early in the investigation, and we can't rule out any possibilities."

"C'mon, Linus. It's me." She held up her hands.

"Okay, sure. That's a logical scenario. And since you brought it up, I would advise you to leave the investigating to me this time."

"I agree," Gary said as he returned to their little confab.

Deena folded her arms and looked at Guttman smugly. "Unless you ask me for my help again."

"I don't anticipate needing it. In other words, don't call me, I'll call you." He turned to walk away, then stopped. "Unless, of course, you come across any new evidence or leads."

Deena nodded.

"I feel so guilty," Estelle said, leaning her head against Russell. "If I hadn't made us come in that stupid car, Leonard would still be alive."

"It's not your fault," Russell said. "You couldn't have known something like this was going to happen."

Deena stood up. "Don't worry, we'll catch whoever did this. They won't get away with it, I promise."

Once again, Deena found herself personally involved in a murder case. So much for leaving the investigation to Guttman.

Chapter 4

OF ALL THE MURDER investigations in which Deena had been involved over the past few years, this one seemed the most cut and dry. Find whoever stole the case full of coins, and you'd bag the bad guy. Another advantage to this case was that the list of suspects was limited to people attending the auction. Of course, with over two hundred attendees, that really didn't narrow down the list of suspects to a manageable number.

Would the thief be a coin collector or just someone who saw an opportunity to steal something of value and make a run for it? And why clobber Leonard in the process?

Deena had some questions for Estelle about Leonard Dietz, but they would have to wait until after church.

Luckily, the Dallas Cowboys were playing the early game, so Reverend Abbott kept the sermon short. If he wanted to see a healthy offering in the collection plate, the good pastor knew better than to keep the fanatics from their football.

"So who do you think might have done this?" Deena asked Gary as they drove to Fitzhugh Manor after services. She had talked him in to a quick stop on the way home, knowing he liked watching games on Russell's new sixty-five-inch smart TV.

"My guess is that it was someone who knew the value of those coins. A collector or an expert, at least. Do they have any surveillance footage to look at?"

Deena chuckled. "Uh, you've been watching too much television. This is Maycroft, not Miami. We're lucky to have stoplights and internet."

"Ha. It's not that bad here. I thought you liked living in a small town."

"I do," she said, "but sometimes I think it might be nice to live someplace with more life—more excitement. You know?"

"And more crime and more poverty."

"And more arts and entertainment."

"Sounds like someone's ready for a vacation," Gary said.

They pulled up to the house and parked in the big circle drive. As Deena walked around the car, her shoe caught on one of the stone pavers, causing her to lunge forward. Luckily, Gary caught her.

"Are you okay?" he asked. "You didn't share some of Penelope Burrows' coffee this morning, did you?"

She inched toward the front porch. "No, it's these darned heels. I don't know what made me think I should wear them this morning."

"Well, you look like a newborn calf taking its first steps."

"Very funny. You try walking on cobblestones in these things."

Deena rang the bell and heard Maggie barking on the other side of the door.

Russell greeted them, but before Deena could barely say hello, he and Gary were hunkered down in matching leather recliners with their feet up and cold beers in hand.

"Estelle's upstairs," Russell called out. "Go on up."

Deena climbed the grand staircase, the same one Estelle's mother, Carolyn, had been pushed down last year at her own Christmas party. The stairway always gave Deena the creeps.

In the middle of the upstairs hallway, Deena saw an open door that led to a spare bedroom where Estelle stored her family treasures. "Estelle?"

"In here," she called, and Deena followed the voice through the open door.

The room was much less packed than Deena had remembered, although one side was still stacked with boxes. Various items were strewn about, some wrapped in newspaper and others covered in layers of dust. She sneezed as though her lungs would fly out of her nostrils.

"Bless you," Estelle said, standing in the middle of the room. She was holding Clover.

"Do you mind?" Deena pointed to the cat.

"Sure," she said and carried Clover out into the hall. "I always forget that you're allergic to cats."

"Thanks," Deena said, rubbing her nose. "So what have you figured out in here?"

"I'm so confused," she said. "When the Johnsons and I were in here last, we made two distinct piles of stuff. One to go to the auction and the other to leave here. When I got back last night after the auction, I found everything in a jumble like you see it now."

"So you hadn't been back in this room before last night?"

"Honestly, no. It was hard going through everything the first time. We had to look at each piece individually, and Patsy and Jeb gave me an estimate of its value. It was so draining."

She pointed across the room. "That side had a lot of the bigger pieces, but there was a clear separation between the two sides."

"When did they move the auction items out of here?"

"About a month ago when Russell and I were in Boston. I guess I should have been here, but I trusted Jeb and Patsy to take care of things. When we finished sorting that day, everything on this side was in boxes and wrapped up."

It was clear that someone had rifled through the boxes and bins. "Who else had access to this room?"

"Well, Russell, of course. But he says he never comes in here. And there's Abby. She's the housekeeper who's been with me for the past few months."

Deena raised an eyebrow.

"I seriously doubt it was her. Why would she make such a mess and just leave it that way? She would know how suspicious that would look."

"Maybe. Is she working today?"

"No, but she'll be here tomorrow."

"I think we should have a talk with her. In the meantime, we should pay a visit to Patsy and Jeb. After all, they were in charge of the auction and were here when everything was moved."

"Okay. I'll get their number and call them. And Deena, I just want you to know how much I appreciate your help. I can even pay you, if you want."

"Don't be silly. We're family."

Estelle left the room just as Deena's cell phone rang. She checked the number and was surprised to see it was Detective Guttman. Yes, because of her work as an investigator, she indeed had him logged in as one of her phone contacts.

"You owe me one," Guttman said, skipping any pleasantries, as usual. "That guy your sister-in-law kicked in the leg at the auction wanted to press charges. Probably thinks he could get a big pay day out of suing a rich gal like that."

"Oh, my. What's his name? I need to warn Estelle."

"Doesn't matter. Anyway, I talked him out of it. Told him she would get a high-priced lawyer and make a fool of him."

Guttman could prove to be a valuable ally sometimes. "That's great. I really appreciate it."

"But there's a hitch. I told him I would recommend she serve some community service time. He seemed to like that. I guess he wanted to see her have to get her hands dirty for a change."

"I see, but just so you know, Estelle is really down-to-earth."

"I have a two-hundred-thousand-dollar Bentley in the police impound lot that says otherwise."

"Fair enough," she conceded, "but driving to the event in that car was unusual. A special occasion."

"Whatever. If I were you, I'd get her volunteering as quickly as possible before the guy changes his mind. Should I call her, or do you want to break the good news?"

"I'll do it. Did you find anything else out from any of the witnesses?"

"Seriously? You're a smart cookie, Deena. You know I can't tell you that."

"I know you *could* tell me, but you *won't*."

"Why do I get the feeling that you're getting involved in this case...again?"

"Because it's personal. And because I'm good at it."

"Are you still working as an investigator for that lawyer, Ian Davis?"

"Actually, I've taken a temporary leave of absence. His wife, Sandra, had her baby, and I'm taking over at the thrift store for her. But that doesn't mean I'm not available to help out if you need me."

"I don't see that happening. But seriously, if you and your sister-in-law come up with anything, you'll tell me about it, right?"

"Sure. *Probably.*"

"Now Deena, you know there's someone out there who wanted those coins—"

She interrupted. "Enough to kill for. Yeah, yeah. I've already heard it from my husband. I don't need to hear it again from you."

"I don't know how that man puts up with you."

Deena had to smile. "I could take that as police harassment, you know."

"I could have had you arrested for interfering with a police investigation at least a half-dozen times, you know. Goodbye, Mrs. Sharpe."

"Bye, and thanks for helping Estelle."

She hung up. *Let's hope there's not another murder in Maycroft when I tell Estelle she's going to be picking up trash on the side of the highway.*

* * *

THE JOHNSONS AGREED to meet Deena and Estelle at the Auction Barn on the outskirts of town. Deena had been there many times before. The exterior of the old structure was plastered with rusty metal signs advertising motor oil and old soda pop. A hitching post for horses and one of those old wooden paneled trucks decorated the front of the building. As a collector and antiques dealer, Deena always got a little tingly going into an auction house or a flea market. You just never knew what you might find.

The Johnson Auction Company was a family-owned business. The eldest son, Leroy Johnson, worked for his parents on the side. He owned several storage facilities in town. He and his buddies also hired out as movers when called upon. It was not uncommon for people in small towns to have several forms of employment to make ends meet.

"Come on in," Patsy said when they came through the door. "I'm glad you called. We need to work out some of the details about what to do with the rest of the auction items."

Jeb appeared from behind a stack of boxes. He reached out his hand to shake. It wasn't the coarse hand of a farmer, but not quite the smooth hand of a man who had spent his life behind a desk, either.

"How are you feeling?" he asked Estelle. "You went through a lot yesterday, what with the breakdown and the death of your butler."

Estelle wrinkled her nose. "First of all, Mr. Dietz wasn't my butler. He was my driver—actually, my mother's driver. And second, what breakdown are you referring to?"

It's funny how some rich people get so defensive about having money.

Taking a step back, Jeb looked at Deena and winked as though they shared some kind of private joke. "Oh, okay. It wasn't a breakdown. I guess you were just a bit 'emotional' about selling off your family's belongings." He made air quotes with his fingers. "I've seen it before. It happens. Don't you worry about it."

The heat rose in Estelle's face. She looked like a teapot about to boil over. "Look here, Mr. Johnson. The reason I took that painting was that it was never supposed to be in the auction in the first place. In fact, there were several items auctioned off that I never authorized you to sell. That's why I got so upset."

Deena nodded, letting him know she was on Team Estelle.

"How could that have happened?" Patsy made a sour face. "We went through the items together. Of course, there were a few things you apparently added after that, but I just thought—"

"I didn't add anything. That's the problem." Estelle crossed her arms, holding her temper at bay. "You said you would leave the items that were stacked by the closet. Clearly, that didn't happen. Why did you break our agreement?"

This side of Estelle was new to Deena. Estelle had gone from a church mouse to a real spitfire.

Patsy's jaw dropped as she looked at her husband.

He rolled his eyes at her. "I knew we couldn't trust him. You said he could handle it."

Patsy rubbed her forehead with the back of her hand. She looked tired and older today.

"What is it," Deena asked. "What's going on?"

Jeb took a handkerchief from his back pocket and blew his nose, an obvious stall tactic. "Leroy. Our son. You see, we had to go out of town for Patsy's aunt's funeral. We left Leroy and his crew to haul everything back here to be catalogued. He must not have listened—as usual."

Patsy headed toward the office area. "Leroy! Get out here!"

The young man strolled into the floor room with his thumbs tucked under the straps of his denim overalls. He had apparently gotten his height from his mama and his girth from his papa. At over six feet tall and pushing two hundred and fifty pounds, he was the kind of country boy you didn't want to mess with.

"What's up?" He glanced past his mother and tipped his John Deere trucker cap in the direction of Estelle and Deena. "Howdy, ladies."

Deena expected Patsy to grab his ear and drag him over like Dennis the Menace.

"What did you do, son, at Miss Estelle's house?" Patsy asked. "You were only supposed to get the stuff on the *right* side of the room, remember? I even wrote it down for you."

Leroy spit on the floor and rubbed it with his boot. "I know how to do my job. It's just not as easy as you think. You made it sound like there'd be stuff over here 'n stuff over there." He used his hands to illustrate. "You never mentioned all the stuff in the middle."

Patsy shook her head. "In the middle? What are you talking about?"

"Maw. There was stuff tossed all over. Looked like a garbage heap, no offense," he said, glancing as Estelle. "I did my best to guess where the middle was."

Jeb turned to Estelle. "Did you go back in there and shuffle things around after we sorted it all out?"

"No. Absolutely not." Although her words were confident, her expression showed doubt.

Jeb lowered his head to peer at her over the top of his glasses. "Well, it sounds like someone did."

They all stood awkwardly. Deena jumped in. "What about the missing coins? Do you have any ideas about who might have taken them right out from under your noses?"

Jeb glanced at Patsy. "We've been doing this a long time. We've had some small lots come up missing after the preview, but never after the auction has started. I'm calling my insurance agent first thing tomorrow to see how much I'm covered for."

Estelle nodded. "Okay, but I'm not as concerned about the value of the coin collection as I am about who stole it. The police think the thief is the same person who killed Leonard Dietz."

"Killed him?" Jeb took a step back as though dodging a punch to the face. "I thought he fell and hit his head. That detective didn't say anything about him getting killed. Anyway, we told him everything we know." He eyed Leroy. "What about you, son, did you see anything suspicious?"

He shuffled his weight back and forth and stared at the ground.

Having interviewed plenty of witnesses as a former reporter and an investigator for a defense attorney, Deena could see that Leroy was hiding something.

"Like I told the cops, I didn't see nothing."

Deena considered pointing out that he had used a double negative in that sentence, which actually meant he did *indeed* see something. She took a more subtle approach. "I'm sure it's hard to keep your eye on everything. You guys had your hands full last night."

"Yes, ma'am."

"Did anyone else notice anything unusual, as far as you know? Was anyone providing security inside the hall?"

More eye darting from Leroy. "Well, Billy was supposed to be keeping his eyes on the room, but..." He glanced down again.

They all waited.

Finally, he finished. "There were a few minutes there when I couldn't find him."

Jeb nearly fell out of his boots. "Couldn't find him? What do you mean?"

"We needed help carrying that big statue, so I called him on the walkie-talkie, but he didn't answer. I looked around and didn't see him. I thought maybe he was in the john, but when he showed back up, I knew he hadn't been."

Patsy asked the question everyone was wondering. "How could you tell?"

Leroy shoved his big hands in his pockets and lowered his head. "Because he smelled like weed."

"Oh, Lordy," Patsy sighed. "I told you not to let that good for nothing leech keep working for you. He's about as useful as a handkerchief in a rainstorm."

"But Maw, we've been friends since we were kids."

"We're running a business here, not a nursery school." Her face took on a blush as she turned back to Estelle. "I'm sorry, Miss Estelle. I don't know what else to say. We were planning on selling the rest of your items at this Saturday night's regular auction. I'll understand if you want to go somewhere else."

"No, that's fine. The sooner the better. I'm ready to put this behind me."

Estelle and Deena turned to leave, and Leroy followed them outside.

He touched Deena's arm and then waited as Estelle got in the car. "You ain't thinking Billy stole those coins, are you?"

"I wasn't, but now I'm wondering if you can be sure he didn't." Deena tried to read his face. It was an honest face this time.

"'Cuz I know he ain't no thief."

"When faced with temptation, we all do things out of character sometimes."

"Not Billy. He has no character."

Deena was pretty sure Leroy didn't realize how that sounded, so she let it slide. "This wasn't the same guy who Estelle, you know..." She made a kicking motion with her foot.

"Naw. That was Randy. He was pissed."

She nodded. "Did you tell Detective Guttman about Billy?"

"No, I didn't think about it until this morning when he didn't show up to help unload the truck."

"We're going to have to talk to him. Maybe he saw something or someone that could be helpful. What's his full name?"

"Billy Ratliff. I don't suppose that would hurt. He lives out on Fletcher. Just don't say anything to my parents. They already hate the guy."

"Fine. I'll see you Saturday night at the auction."

"Yes'um."

As they pulled away, Estelle took out her phone. "Are you thinking what I'm thinking?"

"I'm not sure. What are you thinking?"

"Obviously, someone was in my house and went through that bedroom. The only person it could be is my housekeeper, Abby." Estelle punched in a number. "Abby, I need you to come to my house immediately. I have some questions for you."

As if it wasn't bad enough that Leonard Dietz was dead because of Estelle's auction, now they had a case of domestic pilfering to deal with. Maybe Estelle was just one of those people bad luck seemed to follow.

* * *

ON THE WAY BACK TO the house, Estelle and Deena plotted and strategized their approach with Abby. They chose to go with good cop/bad cop. Estelle would be the bad cop since she could threaten to fire Abby. Deena would be sympathetic and helpful.

Obviously, none of this would be necessary if Abby told the truth when asked, but they both doubted that would happen. But there was a hitch in the plan. Estelle really wanted to hang on to Abby. According to Russell, she made the best barbequed short ribs he'd ever put in his mouth. Sure, they could get another housekeeper who cooked, but some talents are just irreplaceable.

Deena closed off the den, not wanting the boys to get in the way of their plan as they waited for Abby's arrival.

It wasn't long until Deena opened the door and welcomed the poor girl into their trap. "Hi," she said congenially. "I'm Deena Sharpe, Estelle's sister-in-law."

The girl smiled, albeit suspiciously. "Is Miss Estelle here?" Her voice shook a little, making her sound more like a twelve-year-old girl than a twenty-something woman. It didn't help that she had her brown locks pulled back in a ponytail.

"Come on in," Deena said and led her up the stairs.

Abby had put on her maid's uniform, which consisted of a scrub top with her name embroidered on it and a pair of black slacks. She may have assumed Estelle wanted her for an emergency cleaning chore.

At the top of the stairs, Estelle stood in front of the open bedroom door with her arms crossed and a look on her face that would have scared the devil. "Abby, I'm going to ask you a question, and I need an honest answer. Have you been in this room since you started working here?"

The girl swallowed hard. "No, ma'am."

Estelle stared daggers at her. She must have been counting in her head. It seemed like forever before she spoke again. "Are you sure? Think hard, now."

"I'm...sure." The color drained from the poor girl's face, either from guilt or plain old fear.

"As far as you know, has anyone else been in here?"

Abby's eyes darted side to side. That might be her "tell," a sure sign that she was lying. "I saw you in there with some other people. Is that what you're talking about?"

"No. I mean someone else. Maybe your brother or a boyfriend?"

"No, ma'am."

"Well, someone was in here, and I doubt it was a cat burglar."

Tears began to well in the girl's eyes. "I promise you, it wasn't me."

Estelle looked at Deena. "What do you think? Should I fire her?"

Abby let out a groan, which was just the reaction Deena had hoped for.

"Let's not make any rash decisions before we talk to the police," Deena said.

The girl's eyes grew as wide as saucers and her mouth dropped open. She looked like she might spill the beans when her mouth snapped shut.

Deena took her by the arm and led her downstairs. They stood on the front porch.

Abby wiped her eyes with the back of her hand. "Am I in trouble? I've never been in trouble with the police my whole life. Does this have something to do with the auction?"

"News travels fast. Look, I'm sure it will all work itself out as soon as we find out who was in that room. If you know something, you can tell me. I know Estelle likes you. I can talk her into not firing you if you just tell the truth."

Abby looked away and squirmed. "There was this man who came by one day right after Miss Estelle and her husband left town."

Bingo!

"He said he was an old friend and needed to get something from the upstairs study. A book or something." She paused as though hearing her own words made her doubt herself. "I—let him in."

Deena shook her head slowly as though it was a reasonable statement. Inside, though, her stomach did a flip. "Do you know who this man was?"

"No. He told me his name, but I don't remember. It was weeks ago. I didn't know he was going to steal something."

Alarm bells went off. Estelle never mentioned that anything had been stolen. "How long was he here? Did you see where he went in the house or what he did?"

"No."

"What about a description? Do you remember what he looked like?"

"He was older. His hair was kind of gray. Not tall but not short."

"That's it? Anything specific or unusual?"

"No, I wasn't paying much attention."

"Did you see him leave? Did he take anything with him?"

"I was in the kitchen. I never saw him leave." She tugged at the purse hanging from her shoulder.

Deena doubted she was getting the whole story. "Look, I'm going to have to tell the police about this. They'll want to question you."

Abby teetered on her wiry legs.

"It will be fine. As long as you tell the truth, you have nothing to worry about."

"What about my job? I'm supposed to work tomorrow."

"I'm sure it will be fine. I'll talk to Estelle. Just come to work as usual and all will be fine—for now."

"Can you tell her I'm sorry and that I shouldn't have been so stupid?"

Deena put on her high school teacher hat. "We all make mistakes. Learn from it. That's the important thing."

Abby got back in her old blue sedan and waved.

Deena watched her drive away, wondering what it must be like to be in your mid-twenties living paycheck to paycheck. Her heart ached for the girl.

Still, she had to convince Estelle. The good news was that their plan had worked. The bad news was that Deena hadn't yet told her about the impending community service.

Estelle waited in the den. She had apparently filled their husbands in on recent events because the game was muted on the television. "So what did she say?" Estelle asked as soon as Deena popped through the doorway.

"Get this. She said she let a man in who came by saying he was an old friend of the family. He said he was there to retrieve a book or something."

"My word! Did she say who it was?"

"She couldn't remember. She described him as an older gentleman with gray hair and medium height."

"That's not too helpful," Gary said. "I hope you fire her. If she can't be trusted to keep strangers out of the house when you're out of town—"

Deena turned to Estelle. "You can't, not yet anyway. She might know more than she's telling us. Plus, she's the only one who can identify the man."

Estelle paced the room like a prowling cat. "Do you think she was telling the truth?"

Deena let out a sigh. "I'm not sure. Maybe. I had a hard time reading her."

"Do you think whoever came in this house killed Leonard? Maybe there are fingerprints?" Estelle's look turned more hopeful.

"I can ask Detective Guttman, but he'll likely say there were too many people handling those items upstairs."

Gary stroked his chin. "So, do you think a man who knew you were out of town came over to steal the coin collection—presumably—didn't find it but mixed up the piles, then went to the auction, stole the coin collection, knocked Leonard to the ground, killing him, and then got away scot-free?"

"That's how it looks, Sherlock." Deena gave him a thumbs up.

"Hmm. Sounds a little far-fetched to me," he said, and leaned back in his chair.

"Which part?" Russell asked.

"All of it. For one thing, why didn't the guy take the coins when he was here instead of waiting until he was at the auction?"

"Good question," Deena said. "Where was the coin collection when he was here?"

"I gave Jeb and Patsy the coin box and some jewelry to take with them," Estelle said. "The stranger wouldn't have found it because it wasn't here."

"Still," Gary said, "there's nothing to say the two incidents are related."

"You mean the two *crimes*," Deena corrected. "And there's nothing to say they aren't."

Gary looked back at the TV. "Hey, the third quarter is about to start. Can we get home?"

"Sure. Just one more thing." Deena broke the news to Estelle about the call from Guttman and the community service.

She started to protest.

"Sounds to me like you're getting off easy," Russell said. "There's a lot of leeches who would already have a lawyer and be suing for damages by now. I think you should take the deal and thank your lucky stars."

"Maybe," she said reluctantly.

"Hey," Gary said, "the thrift store is a non-profit, right? Does Sandra let people perform community service there?"

Deena's eyes lit up. "Yes! I didn't even think of that. Brilliant!" She looked at Estelle. "Why don't you start tomorrow, and we can plan our next move."

Estelle twisted her face a bit then sighed. "Okay, at least I won't have to wear one of those reflective vests on the side of the road."

Russell laughed. "Or an orange jumpsuit."

Chapter 5

THE CRISP NOVEMBER air rustled the trees, blowing colorful leaves across the road as Deena headed into town Monday morning. Still a week before Thanksgiving, she had barely replaced her Halloween wreath, much less properly decorated the house for holidays.

Hurley, her little black terrier, sat clueless, looking out the back window of the car and barking at pedestrians and other cars. He hated going to the groomer, but he needed his nails trimmed and a bath to get rid of his funky dog smell.

Deena felt a little guilty when she left him at the groomer's even though he was in good hands. He looked up at her with his, "What's going on here?" face when she led him a few doors down from the thrift shop. She promised him he could spend the afternoon with her at the shop to get him to walk in the door.

After saying goodbye, she hurried to the thrift store and turned the sign around to "Open." Still thinking about Hurley, she remembered the day Sandra had brought a small black dog from the shelter to spend the day at the shop. Since the profits from the store went to support the animal shelter, Sandra would volunteer to foster animals that were waiting to get their new "forever homes." Soon after that, Deena adopted Hurley.

He stole her heart with his big brown eyes and black furry face. She named him Hurley after her favorite character from *Lost*.

Mondays at the thrift store were creep fests. After three weeks on duty, she still hadn't gotten comfortable dealing with the death pile. She pulled the key ring out of the register drawer and headed to the large storage closet, wanting to get it over with before any customers showed up.

When she opened the door, an acrid scent of moth balls bombarded her senses, causing her nostrils to flare and her eyes to water. Maybe she had used too many last Monday. She cracked open the window in the smaller room hoping some off the smell would dissipate.

This little ritual was all part of Sandra's superstition. When she had told Deena about the "Clearance Closet," Deena had assumed the room housed clothing to be marked down on sale. Not hardly.

Instead, the small room off the larger storeroom held items that had been recently worn by the newly-deceased. Sandra believed they needed a little time to "clear out the spirit" of the previous owner.

Deena wrote it off as a bunch of nonsense, but she faithfully followed her friend's strict instructions. She gathered up the armful of clothes that were labeled with today's date and carried them out into the shop. They needed a little airing out due to the mothball overkill, so she hung them on a rack in the back. Instead of locking the closet room door, she left it open hoping a cross-breeze would help.

Her favorite part of the day was unlocking the back door to the alley and checking the donation bin for new treasures. The collection box looked like a large wooden post office box, like the kind you drive up to and insert your mail. Of course, it had a larger opening. Sometimes people would leave bigger pieces of furniture or toys next to the box.

Deena unlocked the bin and pulled out several bags of goodies. They felt like they contained clothes, but one made a clinking sound when she carried it. The promise of new treasures gave her a rush. She ripped open the bag. Disappointment replaced hope when she found a bunch of stained baby clothes and three clear glass flower vases from the supermarket.

Luckily, a few customers came by with some promising donations and lifted her spirits.

She prepared price tags for the newly-undead clothing and heard the bell jingle on the front door. Estelle came into the shop with Russell in tow, carrying an armful of ladies' dresses.

"Hey, you two. Whatcha got there?" Deena motioned for Russell to lay the stack across the counter. "Clearing out some of your old clothes?"

"Nope. These were Carolyn's," he said. "I finally convinced Estelle to get rid of them."

Estelle ran her hand across the red velvet jacket on top of the stack. "These are some of Mother's better things. There will be more coming. I figured now was as good a time as any to send them off to new homes."

Deena recognized the jacket. "Isn't this what your mother was wearing when she—died?"

Estelle nodded. "It was one of her favorites."

Uh-oh. This stuff would have to go into the Clearance Closet. That meant Deena would have to tell Estelle about Sandra's superstition. At least they could get a good laugh out of it.

"I'm off to Cliff's," Russell said and kissed Estelle on the cheek. "We're installing a new motor in his RV today. You ladies stay out of trouble." He smiled and left.

"So do I need to clock in or sign something? I want this community service to be official," Estelle said.

"Oh right. I'll give Sandra a call later and find out what we need to do. For now, let's make some coffee so I can tell you about something."

Estelle sat in one of the folding chairs. "Is it about the case? Did you talk to Detective Guttman?"

"Yes. I told him about Abby. He's going to interview her and call me later. But that's not what I want to tell you."

"What is it? Are you naming me employee of the year already?"

"Actually, it's about Sandra and her...um...*system.*"

"*Okay,*" Estelle said, drawing out the word.

"Did I ever tell you about her being superstitious?"

"No, not that I recall."

"Well, she is. Very. One time I opened an umbrella in the shop and she acted like I'd just called on Satan to torch the place." Deena set a cup of coffee in front of Estelle and took a seat at the table.

She blew on the steaming brew. "I'm a little superstitious myself. That would have set me off, too."

"Then maybe you'll relate to this better than I do. You see, Sandra believes that things belonging to people who have just died carry a little of their spirit. Actually, I don't know if spirit is the right word, but you get the point. After they die, the spirit needs time to 'wear off,' so to speak."

"Sure, that makes sense."

Deena had a feeling they weren't going to share that laugh about Sandra's idiosyncrasies after all. "Anyway, she has this separate storeroom where she keeps donated clothes that belonged to people who were recently deceased. Like the clothes you brought in."

Estelle looked surprised. "But Mother's been gone almost a year. Wouldn't they be clear by now?"

Clear? How odd that she used the same word as Sandra. "I'm not sure. I guess I'll have to ask Sandra what her statute of limitation is on ghostly spirits."

Estelle scrunched up her face.

"Sorry. I didn't mean to be indelicate. It's just that I don't believe in all this superstitious hogwash."

"Well, I'd say, better safe than sorry. Let's put Mother's things in that special room just in case." She stood up and marched toward the counter.

Deena followed her, picked up the rest of the stack, and led her to the Clearance Closet. They hung the dresses on the rack where Deena had removed Mr. Carlson's clothes earlier.

"What about other things? Non-clothing items, that is." Estelle looked at Deena as though her question was perfectly normal.

"I'm not sure if the rule applies to hard goods like it does to soft goods. I'll have to ask."

"Good, because I have some more things that aren't going into the auction that I wanted to donate."

Good grief. Why had she opened her mouth? Next thing you know, Estelle would be having an exorcism on Carolyn Fitzhugh's old panty hose and garbage cans. Deena wondered how she kept getting herself into these prickly situations.

* * *

WHO KNEW ESTELLE WOULD be such a retail wunderkind? She talked to customers with ease, gave them her opinion of the clothes they tried on, and mastered the register like a pro.

"I always wanted to be a cashier," she told Deena as she turned all the paper money facing the same direction. "Mother wouldn't let me get a job. Then when I graduated from college and was ready to go out on my own, she had her fall and ended up in a wheelchair. Taking care of her and the staff became my full-time job."

"If you want to work the register, knock yourself out. There's plenty I can do in the back." Deena picked up a stack of empty clothes hangers.

"Oh, thank you!" Estelle said as though she'd just been presented with a new pony. "I just wish it made that cha-ching sound when the drawer opened."

Deena found Estelle's enthusiasm endearing. "By the way, I talked to Sandra," she said. "She said she normally waits about a month to put clothes out after someone has ... passed. Unless—"

"Unless what?"

Deena and her big mouth again. "Unless there's a sign."

Estelle closed the cash register drawer and stared at her. "What kind of sign?"

"I don't know. She just said sometimes unusual stuff would happen, so she'd leave things in the closet a little longer to simmer. Or something like that," Deena said, squirming a little. "Anyway, she said it should be fine since your mother has been gone so long."

"I hope so." Estelle looked toward the front window with a distant look on her face.

Deena hurried to the back, not wanting to drag the conversation out any further. Her cell phone rang. She grabbed it hoping it was Detective Guttman. Instead, it was the dog groomer saying that Hurley was primped and polished and all ready to go.

"I'm going to run down and get Hurley," she said.

Estelle nodded as she wiped down shelves of board games and craft supplies.

Hurley spun in circles when he saw Deena. An orange bandana decorated his neck. "Was he a good boy?" Deena asked.

"He was perfect," the groomer said. "He's all ready for Thanksgiving."

Deena took his leash and led him out the door. "We'll see you next time." She felt like a mother whose kid just made the honor roll.

Hurley pulled her toward the thrift store. It wasn't like he had been there that often, but dogs just have a way of knowing things.

Inside, he ran up to Estelle and threw himself on the ground, belly up. Estelle scratched him and cooed.

He jumped up and ran into the storeroom, obviously re-membering that Sandra kept a big box of dog treats in there.

Before Deena could reach him, he started barking. Loudly. Frantically, even. She worried another mouse would make a surprise appearance. Could it even be a rat? Why had she left that darned window opened?

Estelle followed her back to check out the ruckus.

Hurley had nudged his way into the Clearance Closet, sniffing at everything in sight.

"What is it, boy?" Deena looked around. Not seeing any hairy critters, she tiptoed over and shut the window.

"What's that smell?" Estelle asked as she sniffed the air.

"Mothballs. I guess I overdid it."

"No, that's not mothballs. Believe me, living in that old house, I know what mothballs smell like. It's something else. Pine, I think. Yes, pine."

Deena took in a few whiffs. Estelle was right. The mothball odor had been replaced by the strong smell of pine trees. "Must have blown in from outside. We are near the Piney Woods, you know."

"Blown in? I don't think so. It smells like someone spilled a whole bottle of pine cleaner in here." She bent down to look around the floor.

The bells on the front door jingled, signaling new customers.

"You get that," Deena said. "I'll look for the source of the odor." She moved the rolling racks, looked under a small table, and pushed around a stack of plastic bags. There were no cleaning products to be found. She left the small room and locked the door behind her.

Estelle stuck her head around the corner of the storeroom. "Find anything?"

"Nope. Just a lot of dust."

She cocked her head. "That's odd, don't you think?"

Deena shrugged. "I guess. It's a little unusual."

Estelle's jaw dropped. "Unusual? Maybe it's a sign!"

* * *

LUCKILY, THE STORE got busier, and Estelle didn't mention anything else about signs or spirits or funny smells. Detective Guttman called Deena about his interview with Estelle's housekeeper.

"She gave me the same story she gave you," he said. "Some stranger claiming to be a family friend wanted to look for a book. So she let him rummage around upstairs unsupervised. Right, and I'm the tooth fairy."

"So I take it you didn't believe her."

"It could have happened the way she said, but when I pressed her about why she would allow a stranger into her boss's home, she turned on the tears and clammed up. She's holding something back."

"That's what I thought, too."

"And that description of the man. Older, medium height, gray hair. That narrows it down to just about every geriatric man in town."

"So do you think the two situations are related? Do you think someone was in the house looking for the coins and then stole them from the auction?"

"Possibly, if it happened like she said it did. For all we know she rooted through that room herself or maybe let a sleazy boyfriend in."

"Uh, does she even have a sleazy boyfriend?"

"Don't all single women have them?"

"Oh my," Deena said. "You really need to get out more."

"Maybe if I could find the right—" He stopped, then added, "Never mind."

Deena grinned. "Well, speaking of sleazebags, I have another suspect for us to interview."

"Us? Since when did you get a job with the Maycroft Police Department?"

"Since I came up with another lead. C'mon, Linus. Throw me a bone. It's been weeks since I've stretched my investigative wings."

"If I say yes, will you promise to tell me who it is and let me do the talking?"

"Pinkie swear," she said, holding up her hand next to the phone.

"Regular swearing will do just fine. I'll swing by and pick you up in ten."

Deena hung up, pleased with herself. Now she just needed to convince Estelle to cover for her and take care of Hurley while she went out.

It turned out to be easier than she imagined. Estelle was more than happy to play shopkeeper while she went off to do some sleuthing.

After double-checking the store, Deena went outside to watch for Guttman. As he pulled up, she glanced back at the shop. She knew good and well that the moment they pulled off,

Estelle would be back in that little room looking for more signs from her dead mother.

Chapter 6

UNLIKE MOST SMALL-TOWN police detectives in the South, Guttman always wore a suit instead of the usual khakis and plaid shirt most Texans sported. It may have been a habit from when he worked in Philadelphia. As usual, it was a little wrinkled and about a half size too big. "Where are we going?" he asked.

"The south side of town on Fletcher. We're looking for a Billy Ratliff."

"Got an address?"

"No, but you're a detective, I'm sure you can figure it out."

He rolled his eyes and picked up the microphone for his radio. He called the station for the address. "So what's the story with this Ratliff fellow?"

Deena filled him in on the disappearing act Billy had pulled during the auction. "Even if he didn't do anything, he may have seen something."

"I hope he did. So far, we don't have much to go on. From what the coroner said, it looks like Dietz was hit with a blunt object in the head and fell forward onto the curb. Cracked his skull."

"Could that object be the coin case?"

"Most likely." He sounded his siren to get around a line of cars at the stoplight.

Deena gripped the armrest. She hated driving fast, especially when there was no real hurry. "Does that mean his death would be ruled an accident? Probably the thief didn't intend to kill him."

"That will be up to the district attorney. My guess is it will be manslaughter. It will depend on the evidence, of course."

"What about Mayor Fisk? Did you talk to him?"

"Yep. He says he was inside the whole time. Why? Do you know something?"

"Just that he and a couple of other guys were arguing over by the coin collection earlier in the auction. I thought he may have a lead or hunch or something."

"Huh. He didn't say anything about that. How did you find this out?"

"I saw them when I went to the back of the hall to get a drink." Deena slammed on her invisible brake. "Whoa! Slow down, detective. You don't want to get us killed."

"Sorry." He tapped the brakes.

"I didn't know the other two men."

"What were they talking about? What happened?"

"I wasn't close enough to hear, but I could tell by their faces it wasn't a friendly conversation. A woman dragged off one of the men and they went back to their seats."

"What did they look like?"

"Middle age, maybe older. None of them looked like thieves or killers, if that's what you're asking."

"Do you think you'd recognize them if you saw them again?"

"Maybe. One of them had his back to me, so I didn't get much of a look at him. I think we should talk to Fisk again. I'm sure he would know who they were."

"Definitely." Guttman pulled up to a run-down house that looked like the walls might collapse any minute. "Let's hope this guy's home."

Deena followed the detective to the door, noticing he put his hand on the gun under his suit coat.

This police stuff just got real.

The blaring of a television seeped through the door jamb.

Guttman knocked and waited. He knocked again. "Open up! This is the Maycroft Police Department."

The chain on the other side of the door jangled, and the door creaked open. A guy who looked like he'd just rolled out of bed peeked through the opening.

"Are you Billy Ratliff?" Guttman used his guttural cop voice as he held up his badge.

"Yes sir."

"I need to talk to you. Would you mind stepping outside?"

Why didn't Guttman go inside? It didn't take a blood-hound to recognize the stench of marijuana.

Billy stepped out on the porch, barefoot and shirtless. "What is it, officer?"

"I understand you were working at the auction on Saturday night. Is that right?"

"Uh-huh."

"And at one point you left the building to go to the parking lot. Is that correct?"

The question seemed to revive the young man whose bloodshot eyes grew wider. "Uh, yes sir. I went out to my car. Um, I had to—to get my phone. I left it in my car."

"Your phone." Guttman paused and stared bullets into Billy's brain. After what seemed forever, he asked, "Did you see anything unusual while you were outside 'getting your phone'?"

He didn't actually make air quotes with his hands, but Deena could tell by his voice that he wasn't buying Billy's explanation.

Billy looked at Deena as though she were the good cop.

She puffed out her chest in a show of solidarity but then realized it might just have looked like a flirtatious gesture. She stepped back, hoping to avoid a contact high from the fumes coming off the young man.

"No, I don't think so." Billy crossed his arms and began to shiver as though he just realized summer had turned to fall.

"Are you sure you didn't see anything or anyone?"

He looked down at his arms and put his hands behind him. He may have thought he was about to get cuffed.

"I swear, officer—"

"Detective," Deena said.

"I swear the only person I saw out there was Corey, the security guy."

Guttman pulled about a pad of paper and flipped through the pages. "Corey Rhodes?"

"Yeah, that's the guy. He works security for Mr. Johnson at the auctions."

"I see." Guttman put away the pad. "What happened to your arm?"

Billy looked down as he brought his right arm to the front. It had a large bruise and several scratches. "Oh that. I fell off my motorcycle."

"Fell off your motorcycle," Guttman repeated.

Apparently, the police academy taught its officers to repeat everything like a parrot.

The detective reached in his coat pocket and pulled out his card. Handing it to Billy, he said, "If you happen to think of anything else, give me a call."

Billy let out a sigh of relief—a little too obviously.

But just as he opened the door to go inside, Guttman said, "And Billy, watch out for motorcycles. They can be dangerous."

Deena wanted to give Guttman a standing ovation for the snappy police work. It made for great theater. As they drove off, she asked, "You didn't believe him, did you?"

"Not for a minute."

"And what about his arm? Looks like he might have been in a tussle or a fight."

"That's what I thought. You say he is a friend of the auctioneer?"

"No, a friend of the son's. Leroy Johnson."

"I may have to talk to him. See if he corroborates the story."

Deena nodded, wondering if the Johnsons were right to want to keep their son away from Billy. "Why didn't you bust him for possession? The place smelled like an outdoor concert in the seventies."

"We don't need him for that. We need him for the manslaughter case. I can always threaten him with that later if I find out he's lying."

"Who are we going to interrogate next?" She wiggled in the seat like a child going to Disneyland.

"Unless you have more leads, we aren't going anywhere. I'm taking you back to the thrift store."

"No way! What about Marty Fisk? I know him. I could help you when you talk to him. After all, I'm the one who saw the argument."

Guttman frowned. "Okay, then. Same as before. Let me do the talking unless he says something shady. Just because he's the mayor doesn't mean he doesn't have secrets."

"Like you have to tell *me*. Everybody has secrets, especially politicians."

They drove into town to the Lucky Strike Pawn Shop owned by Mayor Marty Fisk.

She debated telling Guttman about the situation at Estelle's house. It seemed possible that whoever rummaged around in that spare room may have been looking for the coins. Deena glanced at Guttman who seemed deep in his own thoughts and followed his lead.

She didn't have to play all her cards right away. If she held out a bit of info, she could possibly use it to get more details from Guttman later. It's not that she didn't trust him to do a good job investigating on his own, but when it came to figuring out a whodunit, she was better.

At least this time, no one else was in danger of getting hurt.

* * *

THIS WAS THE FIRST time Deena had been back to the pawn shop since she was caught up in a different murder case.

Nothing had changed. The gun case, the shelves filled with small appliances, the musical instruments hanging on the back wall, and the jewelry. She was tempted to look in the glass case but thought better of it. After all, she wanted to instill confidence in Detective Guttman that she could be a valuable asset when it came to solving crimes.

Marty Fisk had the reputation of being a shrewd businessman. That's another way of saying he was one step above a conman. Thus, he had a tendency to get what he wanted.

When he saw Guttman come in, he came straight over to shake his hand like they were good friends. "How can I help you, Detective? Got any leads on those coins?"

As mayor of Maycroft, Fisk was technically Guttman's boss since the mayor reigned over the city council, which hired and fired the police chief. Guttman had probably never seen it that way.

"We were hoping to ask you a few questions about the auction," he said in his usual flat voice.

Deena grinned. Guttman had included her in his "we" statement.

"Sure thing. Come into my office where we can talk in private."

They followed him in and took their seats across from his cluttered desk. Deena noticed several diamond watches and an open box of loose coins. Her eyes stayed on the coins.

"These coins," Fisk said, "they're not the ones from the auction, if that's what you're thinking."

Guttman nodded. "I see. Do a lot of coins come through here?"

"Some. Occasionally."

"I see. I guess that you are somewhat of an expert in rare coins. Is that right?"

"I know a little. Yeah, you could say that." He opened the top drawer and swept the coins in, shutting it with a bang.

"Were you planning to bid on the coin collection at the auction?"

Fisk hesitated as though he might be stepping into a trap. "Uh, yeah, sure. Why?"

"So you must have gotten a good look at them before the auction started. Or, during the auction, perhaps."

Why was Guttman beating around the bush? Why didn't he just ask the names of the three other men involved in the argument? Deena had always interviewed suspects the way she had learned in her journalism training. You get to the point and ask open-ended questions, not these one-word kind. But she kept her mouth clamped. Maybe she could learn a thing or two.

"I got a chance to study them pretty good, but so did everyone else." He studied their faces. "Detective, are you accusing me of stealing those coins?"

"No. Are you confessing?"

"No, of course not." Fisk stiffened. Mr. Congenial had turned into Mr. Defensive.

Guttman grinned. "I didn't think so." He leaned back in the chair.

"The truth is," Fisk said, "that us coin guys were already familiar with this particular collection. A few years before Fitzhugh died, we had started a little club, so to speak. We'd get together and talk about coins and show off our latest finds. After he passed, we stopped getting together. Wasn't much point. As far as I know, there's just three of us coin guys in town now."

"I see. Actually, I have a witness who saw you and a few others having a rather heated discussion at the auction. It appeared to be about the coins. Can you tell me about it?"

Fisk seemed to let down his guard, but only a little. "That's right. The three of us locals were talking about the value of some of the coins when this big shot out-of-towner in a suit comes up and tells us to sit down. We ask him why, and he says it's because we don't stand a chance getting the coin collection. We ask why, and he just stands there with a stupid grin on his face."

"Do you think he was planning on stealing them?" Deena asked, no longer able to bite her tongue. This could be the break they needed.

Fisk cut his eyes at her. "If you were planning to steal something, would you walk up to a group of strangers and announce it?"

"No, I guess not." She slumped down in her chair.

"So what happened next?" Guttman asked, as though Deena were invisible.

At that point, she wished she were.

"You know how it is. We started jawing about how no city slicker was going to come in and take a legacy that belonged in our town and that just because we lived in Maycroft didn't mean we didn't know our way around an auction."

"What did he say?" Guttman took out his pad again. "Did you get his name?"

"Nah, he laughed at us and said he owned three businesses in Detroit and said we were out of our league." Fisk's face reddened. "That's when I told him we needed to talk outside."

"Outside? Did he take the bait?"

"Nah, lucky for him, Clark's wife, Wanda, pulled him away and told us to stop acting like fools and go sit down." Fisk knocked his fist on the desk a few times. "I'd have taken him. You can bet on that."

"I'm sure you would have," Guttman said. "Now who is this Clark?"

"Ronnie Clark. Lives over on Pine. Owns a body shop and the laundry mat."

Guttman made a note. "And who were the other two men?"

"Wyatt Garrison. Retired guy. Used to be a banker." He tightened his fist again. "I don't know the name of that jerk from out of town."

Guttman tapped the pad with his pen. "I know this is tough, but do you think either of the two local collectors might have stolen the coins?"

Fisk swiveled in his chair. "I can't say it hasn't crossed my mind. They're both pretty good guys. Still, you never really know what people will do if a situation presents itself."

"That's for sure," Deena said, hoping to get back in Fisk's good graces. After all, he was the mayor.

Guttman stood up to leave. "I appreciate your honesty, Mr. Fisk. One last question. How much do you think that collection of coins would have sold for? How much is it really worth?"

Deena stood up next to the detective, noting that he said "I" instead of "we" this time.

"Well, that's hard to say." Fisk scratched his chin. "If you've ever been to an auction before, you know that people can get into a bidding war, especially if you want to keep the other fella from winning. But the value of the collection? I'd say close to two hundred thousand."

"That's quite a sum."

"Yeah, but that's not nearly as much as Fitzhugh's other collection. Now, *that* one might be worth killing for." He winked at Deena. "Just kidding, of course."

* * *

GUTTMAN SAID LITTLE on the way back to the thrift store other than to suggest that Estelle should move the second coin collection out of her home and put it in a safe deposit box at the bank.

Deena had gotten used to his silent jags where he seemed to be processing new information. At least he didn't tease her about the dumb question she had asked Fisk.

Could Marty Fisk be right? Hard to believe the second coin collection Estelle had in her safe was even more valuable. If so, who knew about it, and what might they do to get their hands on it?

Hurley wagged his tale and sneezed on Deena's shoes when she came back into the thrift shop. His nose must have been filled with that weird pine odor.

Estelle and Russell were huddled together looking at an old book about the history of Perry County.

"Sorry I took so long," Deena said. "Did everything go okay?"

"Everything was great. I sold that oak table and chairs to a young couple who just moved to town. Luckily, Russell was here to help me load it in their truck."

Russell flexed his arm like Hercules. "The guns are still loaded."

Deena laughed. "Well, you won't believe what I found out." Estelle and Russell were all ears as she told them about the interview with Billy Ratliff.

Russell seemed particularly interested in the part about the motorcycle accident. "Were there any burns on his legs? Were the scratches on his arm normal or did it look like road rash? Did he say if he was wearing leathers at the time?"

"Hold on now, bro. Who's the investigator here?"

"You are, but these are just common abrasions you get when you fall off a motorbike."

Estelle crinkled her nose. "How would you know so much about motorcycle accidents? You told me you hadn't ridden one in years."

Russell turned his pleading eyes to Deena.

She stepped in to rescue him. "I'll keep that in mind when we talk to him again. For now, we are letting him simmer. We're checking some other leads. We went to the pawn shop to have a little chat with Marty Fisk." She described his story about the argument over the coins.

"Who were the two local men involved?" Estelle asked.

Deena wished then that she had taken notes. "Let me see." She stared up at the ceiling as though the names would float down to her from heaven. "Fisk said they used to have some sort of coin collecting club and these two guys were in it."

"Oh, my goodness." A smile crept across Estelle's face. "I hadn't thought of that in years. I remember my father and the other men gathered in the study. They would smoke cigars and talk about their coins. Father would let me stay a while, but I usually got bored and would run off to play. Mother would yell at me not to get my clothes dirty. I remember—"

"Dirty clothes. That's it. One of the men owns the laundry mat. Oh, and the body shop."

"Hmm," Estelle said. "That doesn't sound familiar, although it has been a long time."

"There's a Ronnie Clark who owns a body shop in town. His mechanic helps Cliff and me out sometimes with our *mot*—I mean, trucks."

Estelle closed the book they had been reading and dropped it on the table with a bang.

Deena had a feeling the motorcycle conversation would be continued later at home.

The banging noise jogged her memory. "The other man was retired. I think Fisk said he used to be a banker or a doctor or something."

Estelle turned back to her. "My father knew quite a few of both. Did he say anything more specific?"

"I remember his name made me think of JFK."

"JFK?" Russell looked surprised. "Was it Oswald or Ruby?"

"No. Kevin Costner."

Russell cocked his head. "His name is Kevin Costner, like the actor?"

"No, his name is the same as the guy Kevin Costner played in the JFK movie."

"You mean Jim Garrison, the DA from New Orleans?"

"Garrison. That's it!"

"The way your mind works..."

Estelle held up her hand. "I know a Wyatt Garrison. He used to be my father's banker years ago. Was that the name he mentioned?"

"Honestly, I only remember the last name, but that's probably right."

Estelle's face drained of color.

"What is it, babe?" Russell asked. "Are you okay?"

She nodded slightly. "I just thought about what Abby said...about the stranger."

"What?" Deena asked. Estelle looked as though she'd just seen a ghost. And in Estelle's case, the possibility was real.

"Wyatt Garrison is one of our oldest family friends."

Deena gasped. "You don't think he was the one who came to the house claiming to look for a book, do you?"

She shook her head. "Impossible. We've known the Garrisons for years. He was like family. In fact, I used to call him Uncle Wyatt. He taught me how to play chess."

"Then why have I never heard of this 'Uncle Wyatt'?" Russell asked.

Estelle clenched her hands together. "After Father passed, he and Mother had a falling-out. I'm not sure what it was about. Knowing Mother, it was probably something silly. We haven't been in contact with him for years." She stopped and looked down, whispering, "Bless her heart."

"Don't you think we should say something to Detective Guttman?" Deena asked.

"No. Absolutely not. If he should check into anyone, it should be that other man. The body shop owner." She looked up at Russell and glared, apparently remembering the motorcycle comment. She got up and went straight to the storeroom.

Deena looked at Russell, who appeared equally confused.

Had this discussion sent Estelle over the edge?

"We better check on her," Russell said.

Deena followed him to the back with Hurley once again on her heels.

Estelle, frozen as though caught between reality and fantasy, stood in the doorway of the Clearance Closet. Deena followed her gaze into the room and saw what looked like a scene from a movie. The orange glow of the setting sun beamed through the window as feathers floated and danced around the room, slowly making their way to the floor.

"What on earth?" Deena couldn't imagine what had happened.

As the three of them watched the surreal sight, Estelle finally spoke. "It's a sign."

Chapter 7

THOSE WHO LIVE in big cities seem to believe that everyone in small towns knows everyone else. That's a myth. Besides the fact that you can never *really* know another person, small town people have their cliques just like big city folks. What *is* true, however, is that small town people tend to be more suspicious of strangers. That certainly was the case in Maycroft.

As Deena drove home, she couldn't stop thinking about Wyatt Garrison. After Estelle's initial freak-out, she totally dismissed the possibility that he could be involved in the case. Estelle even made Deena promise not to disclose to Guttman the fact that he had a relationship to the family. Deena didn't like it, but she really had no choice.

And what about those feathers? Tomorrow she would investigate the source first thing. Rather than entertain Estelle's notion that they were a sign, Deena had just closed the Clearance Closet door declaring that it had been a long day and that they all needed to go home.

Deena glanced at Hurley in the seat next to her. He still had a few of the small flurries stuck to his face from when he tried to catch them in his mouth like snowflakes.

As she turned into her suburb of Butterfly Gardens, she realized she had forgotten to ask Estelle about the second coin collection. Should she give her a call? Glancing at the clock, she realized the banks were already closed. Estelle couldn't take the collection to the bank and put it in a safe deposit box tonight anyway. For that matter, it might already be there. It could wait until tomorrow. They'd had enough drama for one day.

Speaking of drama, Deena saw Christy Ann with her oldest boy walking up the street pulling a wagon. What could she be selling this time? If nothing else, growing up in the suburbs trained kids how to be little entrepreneurs. Every time you turned around they were selling some overpriced candle or cookie dough to support their team or club or church or what have you.

Deena pulled into the driveway and let Hurley out of the car. He ran up to little Davey and rolled over for belly scratches. Davey squealed with delight.

"Hey, Deena. You look like you've had a rough day."

Ahh, Christy Ann. You could always count on her to make even the simplest pleasantry sound snarky.

"Yes, it has been. What's your excuse?"

She laughed as though Deena were surely kidding.

Christy Ann, a typical suburban, stay-at-home mom, could always be trusted to give Deena a run for her money. Who knows what went on behind closed doors, but in front of them, Christy Ann always looked refreshed and put together like someone on the cover of one of those parenting magazines they have at the dentist office.

"You're such a delight, Deena. Isn't she, Davey?"

Deena ruffled. Sounded like code for "we can't stand her but we're smiling anyway." Deena glanced in the wagon. Cookies. Boxes and boxes of cookies.

"Looks like another fundraiser," Deena said. "What is it this time? Buying kittens for sick children or sending toddlers to space camp?"

Christy Ann literally tisked at Deena. "It's for the youth soccer league. Don't you remember me telling you that Davey made All-Stars?"

"All-Stars? How old is he? I thought he just barely learned to walk."

She shook her head. "I know it's hard for people who are childless to understand, but Davey is five and he's a gifted athlete."

Childless. She might as well have called her a barren waste of space. As much as Deena loved her friendly banter with her favorite neighbor, exhaustion was beating on her door. She wanted to get inside. "Just tell me how much they are and how many I need to buy," she said, reaching for her wallet.

"Actually, if you buy a case, I can give you a discount. Only five dollars a box."

"What am I going to do with a case of cookies? I'm on a diet."

"Ooh, that's good to hear. Well, you could always freeze them. You can thaw them out and take them to a party and pretend you baked them."

That was a low blow. Christy Ann knew her too well.

"I'll have you know that Gary's mother taught me how to make Hello Dollies using her super-secret cookie recipe."

"And how many batches of those have you whipped up?"

"Touché. Give me a case. Maybe I can sell some to the customers at the thrift store."

Christy Ann tilted her head like Hurley when he didn't quite understand something. "I didn't know you were having to shop at the thrift store, although I should have guessed. You and Gary aren't having financial troubles, are you?"

"No, not that it's any of your business. I'm filling in for my friend Sandra who just had a baby. That's what us 'childless' people do."

"That's a relief."

Deena handed her the cash and took the large case of cookies. "Good luck with soccer, Davey. Hope you win the biggest trophy they make." She opened the back door of her SUV and tossed in the box. Under her breath, she added, "So I can clobber your mother with it."

Chapter 8

ESTELLE WAS ONE of those perky morning people Deena couldn't stand. Even as a teacher, Deena had always had a hard time trying to appear chipper and raring to go with her first period class. It helped that Estelle showed up with Deena's favorite mocha caramel latte.

"So, what's on the agenda for today?" Estelle asked. "Do we have new inventory to price and put out? I just love using the pricing gun."

"Easy there," Deena said. "Let me get my sea legs first." She plopped down in a chair and put her feet up on a box.

"I'm just excited to be here. It's so much fun to work in a store. Do I need to get money out of the safe to put in the register?"

Deena took a gulp of coffee. "What do you think this is, a bank? There's no safe. I took the money bag home with me last night. It's in my black satchel." She looked over at the table where she had set her purse. No bag.

"Oops. Must have left it in the back of my car."

"I'll get it," Estelle said and reached in Deena's purse for the keys.

If she was going to be this energetic, Deena might have to find her another place to do the rest of her community service.

Estelle came back in carrying the bag and a box of cookies. "You bought a whole case of cookies? I thought you were on a diet."

"I am." She explained how Christy Ann had ambushed her.

"Let me bring a few of them in from the car. We'll set up a little display on the front counter. I'll make a sign." And off she went.

Good. That should keep her busy at least a few minutes. The coffee cleared some of the fog in Deena's head. She looked around at the bags and boxes of clothes that seemed to have multiplied since yesterday. Estelle must have gotten some more drop-offs when Deena was out of the shop with Guttman.

That reminded her of his warning about the second coin collection. When Estelle returned to get some paper to make her sign, Deena motioned for her to have a seat. "I need to ask you about something Marty Fisk said about your father. He mentioned that the other coin collection you have is even more valuable than the one that was stolen. Did you know that?"

"I never thought about it. I just know that they were very special to my father. That's why I'm keeping them for now."

Alarm bells rang in Deena's head. "Where did you say you keep it?"

"It's in the safe. I keep all my valuables in the safe now."

"Do you know how much it's worth?"

"I have no idea."

Deena turned down the thermostat. Between hot flashes and hot coffee, sweat dripped from her hairline. "Well, according to Fisk, they are worth a lot of money. In his words, 'They might be worth killing for.'"

A tremor made its way through Estelle's body. "Oh dear. Do you think I'm in danger? What should I do?"

"Detective Guttman suggested you put the coins in a safe deposit box at the bank."

"Okay. That will keep the coins safe, but what about me?"

"Let's see where Guttman is on his investigation. I'll call him and see if he can come here to meet with us." She patted Estelle's arm. "Now, finish up with the cookie display so you can fire up the pricing gun. We have a lot of work to do."

* * *

FOR SOME REASON, MORE merchandise was coming into the store than going out. One customer had come in looking for tablecloths and a few others were shopping for Thanksgiving décor. Several people dropped off donations.

When the bell jingled on the front door, Deena walked out of the storeroom to see Detective Guttman staring at a used motorcycle helmet.

"Howdy, Detective," Deena said. "Don't tell me you ride?"

"Sure I do. And I don't think this old helmet is up to code. Make sure to tell whoever buys it not to wear it for protection."

"Will do." She picked up the helmet and called for Estelle to join them.

"I just got off the phone with Russell," she said. "He's going to take the coins to the bank for me. Detective, do you think someone might come to my house looking for the second collection?"

"I'm no fortune teller, but there's always that possibility."

She looked at him with wide eyes. "What should we do?"

"Make sure you lock your doors and keep your security system on, especially at night. You do have one, right?"

"Yes. Russell had one installed right after we got married."

"I can make sure the department patrols your neighborhood. It's unlikely that the thief will strike twice, but you can never be too cautious."

Estelle's face dropped even farther.

"How about some cookies, Linus?" Deena asked, trying to shut him up. "Just five dollars a box." She started piling boxes in his arms as he protested.

"Now Deena, you know us cops prefer doughnuts." He stacked the boxes back on the counter. "I guess I can take one, though." He took the money out of his wallet and slapped the cash on the counter. He looked back at Estelle. "By the way, have you gotten anything else out of that housekeeper of yours?"

Estelle had zoned out.

Deena snapped her fingers in front of Estelle's face like a hypnotist reviving his victim. "Estelle. Detective Guttman asked you a question."

"Oh, um, no. She's still saying a stranger came to the house. Do you think she's lying?"

"Maybe. Be sure to drop it to her that the other coins are now at the bank, just to be on the safe side. This is a small town. Word will get around."

"I could mention it to Penelope Burrows," Deena said. "Then everyone will know. What about the two men from the coin club that Fisk mentioned? Have you talked to them?"

"Not yet. There's a security guard I want to talk to first. According to the auctioneer, he was patrolling the parking lot. He told the police he didn't see anything suspicious, but I want to see if I can shake his memory a little."

"Can I come?"

"Deena, I don't want to be here alone." The color began returning to Estelle's face. "Please stay here with me."

"You're right," Deena said softly. "I wasn't thinking."

Guttman cut his eyes at her. "It wouldn't matter anyway. I already got a chewing out from the Chief about taking you with me to see Marty Fisk. Apparently, Marty Fisk still holds a grudge against you."

"That really isn't surprising since I did reveal that he was cheating on his wife."

"I was told in no uncertain terms that I was not to include you in the investigation of this case or any other if I want to keep my badge. And yes, I want to keep my badge."

"Hmm. Maybe if I talk to Fisk, I can change his mind."

Guttman looked as though he might blow. "Mrs. Sharpe, this is my job we're talking about."

Deena crossed her arms. "Detective Guttman, this is my family's safety we're talking about." She glanced back at Estelle and shook her head. "I'm sure it's going to be fine."

Estelle just stared at the floor.

Guttman let out a guttural sound. "Well, you ladies stay out of trouble, you hear?" He turned and left the shop.

"Not hardly." Estelle snapped back to life. Deena followed her as she marched straight to the storeroom and picked up the shop keys. She unlocked the closet door and opened it slowly. The feathers once again floated in the air.

"What are you doing?" Deena asked.

"Seeing if I get another sign."

Where had all those darn feathers come from? Deena pushed around some of the clothes on the rack. She found the culprit. Apparently, something had chewed a large hole into a down-filled jacket. "Look," she said, showing the coat to Estelle. "It must have been a mouse. When you opened the door, the air stirred up the fallen feathers."

Deena wasn't sure that having mice was more comforting than the thought of a ghost. She looked around for more signs of the critter.

Estelle seemed undeterred by the discovery. She ran her hand across her mother's clothes, whispering under her breath.

Just then, something clattered to the floor, causing both women to jump. It was a small silver bell.

"Look!" Estelle picked it up. "It's one of Mother's bells! The ones she used to ring when she called for me or the housekeeper. It's another sign!"

That was the last straw. "Estelle, there are no such things as signs from your dead mother. I'm sorry if that sounds harsh, but get real. There are no ghosts or spirits or any other superstitious nonsense going on in here."

"How do you know? Sandra thinks so, and this is her shop."

Saved by the bell. Actually, it was the ringing of Estelle's cell phone. She walked out of the closet to take the call.

Deena locked the door behind her and shoved the keys in her pocket.

"That was Russell," Estelle said, picking up her purse. "The bank won't let him open the safety deposit box. They said I have to do it. I'm going to drive over there."

"Good. I mean—that's fine. You can even take the rest of the day off if you want."

Estelle tilted her head. "You're not getting rid of me that easy. I'll be back after lunch."

Deena let out a sigh as the front door jingled as she closed it behind her. Time to take matters into her own hands. She wanted to call the auction house and get the name of that security guard. She didn't need Guttman's permission to ask questions of her own.

But first, she needed to call an exterminator. As she looked up the number of Bugs-Be-Gone, she wondered if the shop actually needed an *exterminator* or an *exorcist*.

Chapter 9

INSTEAD OF TAKING the risk that she might run into Guttman at the Auction Barn, Deena follow a hunch and drove south to Billy's place. Several trucks and a motorcycle lined the street in front of the house. Before knocking, she wrapped her hand around the small can of pepper spray in her purse.

Billy opened the door. His eyes were bloodshot, but at least he was fully clothed this time. "Hey. You again."

"Yes, Deena Sharpe. I was hoping to ask you a few more questions."

He came out to the porch and shut the door behind him. "What is it now?" His long sleeves covered his bruised arm, but she could still see scratches on his hand. He smelled like he'd been to a Stones concert .

"Billy, I'm worried about you," she said, taking a page out of her teacher handbook. "I'm worried you're hiding something from the police and it's going to get you in trouble. And I'm not just talking about the drugs."

He swallowed hard and folded his arms defensively. "What do you want to know?"

"How did you really get hurt? Those abrasions weren't caused by a motorcycle fall." She hoped the observation would give her some street cred.

He blinked his eyes and shoved his hands in his jeans pockets. "I—I got side-swiped by a car—at the auction."

"What do you mean? How?"

"I had been smoking in my car. When I crossed the drive to go back to the building, a car came screaming past me and hit my arm."

"Why didn't you tell anyone?"

"I wasn't supposed to leave the auction. I didn't want to get in trouble. The Johnsons are always looking for a reason to fire me."

"Did you get a look at the driver or the car?"

"I wasn't paying attention, so I didn't see the driver. It was a black car. That's all I remember."

"A black car. Was it a sedan? An SUV? Anything specific?"

"No. I just remember that my arm ached like the dickens. The side mirror must have caught me."

He seemed to be telling the truth. "What about a security guard? Was there someone else in the parking lot who might have seen the car?"

"Corey was on security duty that night. He had been with me at my car, but had gone off in a different direction."

"The security guard was at your car?"

"He and I are buddies. He came by for, well, you know." He put his fingers to his mouth as if taking a drag off a cigarette.

That explained a lot. Maybe the security guard didn't see anything because he was busy getting high with Billy. "Can you tell me where to find your friend Corey?"

Billy drew his shoulders back and clamped his mouth shut.

"Look," Deena said. "I can talk to Jeb Johnson or you can tell me where to find him and we can hopefully keep this between us." She clutched the pepper spray tighter behind her back.

Billy let his gaze drift toward the front door. "If I tell you, you won't say anything to the cops, will you?"

That was an easy one to answer, knowing Guttman was probably just one step behind her. "No, I won't."

"He's in the house. Let me get him."

Before she could say anything, Billy had disappeared inside. *This is it, Deena. This is where the bad guys come out with guns blazing and the amateur sleuth ends up in a shallow grave outside of town.*

She took a few steps back and got out her cell phone. She punched in a nine and a one, waiting with her trigger finger hovering over the last number. Despite the cold wind, sweat formed in her pits.

The door opened slowly as a young man in his early twenties stepped outside.

"Corey Rhodes, is that you?" she asked.

"Hey, Mrs. Sharpe. You remember me." He smiled.

"Of course I do." Dropping the phone in her purse, she reached out to shake his hand. "You were one of my favorite photography students. So what are you doing here?" She tried not to look too disgusted by her surroundings.

"Oh, just hanging out with some friends."

"I thought you went off to college."

"I did. I dropped out. Too much partying and not enough studying. But I'm taking classes at the community college now."

"That's good. What are you studying?"

"Criminal justice."

"Corey, there are drugs in there. You do realize —"

"I know," he said. "I should know better than to hanging out here." He dropped his chin to his chest.

"What would your mother think if she knew you were over here? She's a parole officer, right?" Deena didn't wait for an answer. "Well, I won't say anything to your mother, if you answer some questions for me."

He looked up. "My mom would kill me if she knew I was hanging out with Billy. Ask me anything."

"What did you see on the night of the auction? Did you see Leonard Dietz or who ran into Billy?"

"I had been walking around. I noticed the old man—Dietz—sitting in his car. I nodded and he nodded back. I had been walking back and forth when I saw Billy come outside. I followed him to his car. But before I did, though, I glanced back and saw the old man standing next to his car talking to somebody. I probably should have gone over there..."

"But you didn't."

He nodded his head.

"Did you get a look at the person?"

"No. They were too far away. It was just someone wearing a long coat with a hood. Honestly, I couldn't even tell you if it was a man or a woman. They seemed to be talking. I just assumed they knew each other."

"Did you tell this to the police when they questioned you that night?"

"No. I was too scared, you know. I was supposed to be keeping the cars safe and somebody got killed. I guess I should go to the police and tell them." He looked down at his feet.

"Well, I have a feeling you will get your chance pretty soon. A detective is looking for you to ask you some questions. You have to promise me you'll be honest."

"I promise."

She pointed to the house. "Now go in, get your things, and go home. I don't want to find out you've been back here again."

"Yes ma'am." Corey turned to the house but stopped. "Mrs. Sharpe, why are you so interested in this case? I thought you were just a teacher."

Deena tried not to react to the word "just." "Not anymore. Leonard Dietz was my sister-in-law's chauffeur."

"I'm really sorry." He opened the front door. Before he closed it, Deena saw several other people inside. They looked up and squinted as the light poured in and flooded the dark room.

Sitting on the sofa next to Billy was Leroy Johnson. He had his arm draped across the shoulders of a girl. It was Estelle's housekeeper, Abby.

Chapter 10

SINCE SHE WASN'T WORKING for the newspaper as a reporter or for Ian Davis as an investigator, Deena realized she had no obligation to keep the information she uncovered or the source of that information confidential.

However, she had promised not to tell Corey's mother that he was hanging out with Billy. She'd also promised Billy she wouldn't say anything to the police. Guttman would likely find out everything on his own anyway.

A part of her felt like driving straight over to tell Jeb and Patsy just what their son Leroy was doing and find out if they knew about his relationship with Abby. As a teacher, she always had to walk a fine line between keeping a student's trust and watching out for his or her best interest, not unlike the position she was in now. This time, though, Estelle and Russell were her first priority.

As she drove back to the shop, questions swirled in her head. Why would Leroy be hanging out with Abby? Were they in on something together? Had Abby been at the auction Saturday night?

Maybe Estelle could help figure out Abby's role in all this.

Once again, Deena had forgotten to eat. She picked up a box of sugar cookies and carried it into the store. She missed Hurley. He would have loved a cookie.

Maybe she would start bringing him to the shop every day to keep her company. Besides, he could also scare away the mice. After all, terriers had been bred to burrow for rodents, which is probably why he spent so much time chasing squirrels in the backyard.

She was halfway through the box of cookies when Estelle came rushing in the door. "I've got it! I know what the sign means!" She breathed heavily as though she had run back to the store on foot.

"Oh brother." Deena started to protest when Estelle held up her hand.

"Just listen," she said. "There were three clues. The pine smell, the feathers, and the bell. What do they all have in common?"

"Um, they're all in your imagination?"

"No! They all have to do with Abby."

Abby? How ironic. Deena had planned to ask *her* about Abby. "How do you figure?"

She counted off the clues on her fingers. "Abby is my housekeeper. She uses a strong-smelling pine cleaner."

Deena waited for more.

"She also uses a feather duster. *Feathers*."

"That's a stretch, but okay."

Estelle put her hands on her hips. "And, you know good and well that Mother used those little silver bells to summon the maid. *Always*. Mother is trying to tell me something about Abby. I think Abby could be the thief and the killer."

Goosebumps popped up on Deena's arms. She didn't want to admit it, but Estelle's point had an eerie, logical ring to it. "Well, putting all of your 'solid evidence' aside, I have some suspicions of my own about Abby."

Deena told her about the visit with Billy.

Estelle hung on every word. "So you think whoever stole the coin collection must have been an acquaintance of Leonard's and ran into Billy as he *or she* was escaping the scene?"

"Looks that way. Oh, and the person was driving a black car."

"It was Abby. I know it. Especially now that we know she is in cahoots with Leroy. I say we call Detective Guttman now."

"Hold your horses. All we have right now is a hunch and a sign from your dead mother. We're going to need more than that for Guttman to take us seriously."

"What do you suggest then?" Estelle asked. "We could go Jack Bauer on her and torture it out of her."

"Whoa. This is America, remember? And we're not rogue CIA agents. Although, that does give me an idea."

"What? I was just kidding about the torture, you know."

"The best way to squeeze the truth out of a witness or a suspect is to catch them in a lie. We need to get two vital pieces of intel from her."

Estelle's eyes lit up as she rubbed her hands together. "I love it when you talk like a P.I."

"We need to know where she was on Saturday night, and, assuming she has an alibi, who the stranger was that she claims came to the house."

"Ooh! You sound just like one of those television cops. Sunday night has the best mystery lineup, in my opinion. So, what's your plan?"

Deena stewed a minute. "Lineup. That's it! Get our purses and follow me. We're closing the shop to chase down a suspect. If this plan works, Detective Guttman will have to eat his words." She called the newspaper office and got the information she needed.

Estelle returned just as Deena hung up. "Who was that?"

"Oh, just a friend. I still have my connections at the newspaper, you know. He's texting me an address." They got in the car and waited for the message.

"Tell me about this lineup. Are we going to the police station?"

"No. We're going to prepare a photo lineup. Abby said the man who came to the house was older, medium height, graying hair. We know the three men who were arguing over the coins were Garrison, Clark, and Fisk. We need to get pictures of them."

"Fisk talked to us about the coins at the auction. I don't think he's guilty," Estelle said.

"Neither do I. Besides, he has dark hair and is built like a tank. That leaves Clark and your friend Garrison."

Deena's phone dinged and she read the address. "That's it. We're off."

"I haven't seen Wyatt Garrison in years, and I certainly wouldn't call him a friend after all this time. I wish I knew what he and Mother had argued about that caused such a rift."

"We're going to talk to Ronnie Clark first. Hopefully he'll be home or else we'll have to track him down at work."

"But you said we need a picture of him. How will we get it?"

Deena lifted her cell phone. "I'll take it with this."

"Oh, so we are going to his house and saying, 'You don't know us from Adam, but we were wondering if you stole my father's coin collection and killed my driver. And also, can we take your picture?'"

"Not exactly." Estelle had a point.

Deena turned down the street and found the house. "Nice digs. There's obviously good money in smashed cars and dirty clothes."

When she got out of the car, Deena glanced in the back seat. A plan hatched. "Grab some of those cookie boxes. I have an idea."

They walked up the stone-covered path to the front door, each of them carrying an armload of boxes. Deena rang the bell.

A woman answered the door. "Hello there."

"Hi. We're selling cookies and wondered if you would like to buy some."

The woman wrinkled her nose and stared. "Aren't you two a little *old* to be selling cookies door to door?"

Estelle held out a box. "They are for a good cause. Is your husband here? Maybe he'd like some."

As she eyed the two women suspiciously, Deena felt like a creeper trolling for children. "Like we said, they're for a good cause. They're for the—"

"Library," Estelle said just as the words "animal shelter" came out of Deena's mouth.

"The animal shelter library?" The woman folded her arms across her chest.

Deena attempted to explain. "Um, yes. The books are for the animals, I mean people, not the dogs. Dogs can't read. Obviously."

"Deena Sharpe, are you drunk?" the woman asked.

Deena felt her mouth drop open. *Who is this woman and how did she know my name?*

"Wanda," a voice from behind her called. "Who is it?"

"It's Mrs. Sharpe and some woman," she hollered back, staring at Deena's puzzled face. "Obviously, you don't remember me. You taught our Kevin. He graduated about fifteen years ago."

"Kevin Clark," Deena said aloud, turning the name over in her brain. It didn't click, but that didn't stop her from saying, "Oh, right. I remember. How's he doing?"

A man stuck his head around the corner. "What in tarnation is going on here?"

Wanda motioned toward her. "You remember Deena Sharpe. She was Kevin's journalism teacher."

"Ronnie Clark," he said, and offered his hand.

"Hi, this is my sister-in-law, Estelle." Deena thought it best to leave off the last name for now. She didn't know if the name "Fitzhugh" would raise a red flag.

"Where are my manners," Wanda said. "Won't you two come in out of that cold wind?"

They stepped inside. Deena handed her cookie boxes to Estelle to free up her hands to use the camera on her phone.

"So, let's take a look at these cookies," Wanda said. "They look yummy."

"Wanda, I have to get back to work. Nice to see you ladies." Ronnie nodded and maneuvered around them to the front door.

"Wait," Estelle said. "Weren't you at the auction Saturday night?"

Uh-oh. Deena had no idea where her sister-in-law was going with this.

Ronnie pulled his car keys out of his pocket. "Um, yes. Why do you ask?"

Estelle swallowed hard. "I understand you knew my father and were interested in his coin collection."

As if frozen, he stared back at Estelle. "Are—you—Donald Fitzhugh's daughter?"

"Yes," she said with the faintest of smiles.

"I didn't recognize you. You were all dolled up the other night at the auction."

"Yes, well, I was wondering if you knew who might have stolen my father's coin collection. Was it you?"

Oh my. Nothing like ripping the Band-Aid off.

"What the—"

Deena tried to salvage the situation. She still hadn't gotten a picture of him. "Look, she didn't mean that. What she meant to say was—"

"I know what she meant! She thinks I'm a common thief. What do you want to do? Search me? Do I look like someone who needs to steal to pay my bills? You people are crazy!" With that, Ronnie Clark stormed off.

"Ronnie!" Wanda started after him, but then stopped. She sucked in a deep breath and shook her head. "How dare you come to my home and accuse my husband of such a thing?"

Estelle looked like a water balloon about to burst.

"This has all been a misunderstanding," Deena said. "If you'll just let me explain. Wanda, please."

"I guess so," she said and led them to the formal living room. "Come have a seat. Set those boxes on the table." She grabbed a tissue and handed it to Estelle whose eyes were beginning to leak tears.

Through the front bay window, they could see Ronnie Clark pulling out of the driveway and racing down the street. Sure enough, his car was black.

Deena noticed a row of family pictures on top of the baby grand piano. She picked up one of the pictures and had a vague recollection of the young man she had taught so many years before. "Is this Kevin and his children?"

"Yes," Wanda said proudly. "That was taken last year at Christmas."

"Beautiful family." She set the frame back down and took a seat on the sofa next to Estelle.

Wanda wrung her hands. "I want to apologize for Ronnie's outburst. I know how that must have sounded."

Ya think? The man practically confessed.

"No, it's me who should apologize," Estelle said. "It's just been such a trying few days."

"I can imagine," Wanda said. "Still, that was no excuse for Ronnie to yell like that. It's just that, well, he has a bit of a problem. Sometimes his temper..."

Red flags went up. Could Ronnie Clark be an abusive husband?

Wanda must have read their minds. "Oh, it's not that. It's just that..."

"You don't have to explain." Deena looked around, wondering how they were going to get out of this mess.

"No, it's just that—he drinks—and sometimes he loses his temper, you know? Terrible, but whatcha gonna do?" She shrugged her shoulders. "He's a good man and would never steal from anyone. In fact, he doesn't even collect coins any more. Let me show you." She jumped up and motioned for them to follow.

"That's not necessary," Estelle protested and turned to Deena.

Grabbing her by the arm, Deena whispered, "Keep her busy while I take a picture of one of these photos of Ronnie."

Estelle nodded. "Oh, what an interesting room," she said, trailing Wanda into the den.

Deena snapped a couple of quick shots of photos of Ronnie and Wanda that were sitting on top of the piano, then hurried to the den.

The room's décor starkly contrasted the formal front room with its mahogany tables and flowing curtains. The pine-paneled den looked like a hunting lodge complete with a stuffed turkey and a jack-a-lope, a Texas favorite. There were more animals on the walls than at the Perry County Zoo.

Deena had never seen so much taxidermy in one place. "Wow," she said, trying to take it all in.

Wanda beamed. "Isn't it beautiful? This room is our pride and joy." She crossed over to a bank of built-in cabinets and pulled out a magazine. "Look, we were featured in *Country Homes* magazine a couple of years ago." She flipped through the pages and showed them the spread.

"That's impressive," Deena lied. She hated the idea of some-one shooting Bambi's mother. But as a Southern gal, she had gotten used to it. "My brother Russell would be right at home here, right, Estelle?"

She nodded her head. "You know it."

Deena handed the magazine back to Wanda.

"No, no. You keep it. I have lots of them. You can show it to your brother."

"Thanks."

They stood awkwardly waiting for Wanda to say some-thing.

"Oh! I almost forgot." She walked over to a huge safe, the kind hunters liked to keep their guns locked up in. She pushed in a code on the front panel, it clicked, and she opened it. "See? No coins."

Deena stared at the contents. A rifle, a few stacks of paper, several boxes of what appeared to be ammunition. "You're right."

"Well, I guess we should be going," Estelle said, walking back into the living room. She scooped up the boxes of cookies. "Again, I want to apologize for the intrusion."

"No need, honey," Wanda said. "I understand what can happen when you're under such stress."

"It was nice seeing you again," Deena said.

"Wait! Let me buy a couple of boxes of those cookies from you. It's the least I could do."

"Don't be silly," Deena said. "Take whatever you want."

"Thanks." She took two boxes. "Ronnie just loves peanut butter crunch."

As soon as they had driven a safe distance away, Deena turned to Estelle. "Oh my gosh! I think Ronnie Clark stole those coins."

Chapter 11

ESTELLE URGED DEENA to head straight to the police, but Deena still wanted hard proof. Besides, they still didn't know what role Abby may have played in the crime. They also wanted to clear Wyatt Garrison of any suspicion. The best way to do that was proceed with their plan to get pictures to show Abby and see if she identified any of the men as the stranger she let pillage Estelle's house.

"I'm sorry I cracked up back there," Estelle said. "I was worried Ronnie Clark would leave, and we wouldn't get a picture of him. I guess I better leave the questioning to you this time."

Deena waved her off. "You did fine, don't worry. We just need to figure out how to approach Garrison. I think the 'sixty-something Girl Scout cookie salesman scheme' is out. Plus, he will recognize you, I am sure."

"That's true." Estelle pointed for Deena to make a right-hand turn.

"What if we take the 'concerned friend' approach? You could say that you heard he was under investigation and you wanted to check on him."

"That could work. Besides, it's practically the truth."

"I could offer to take a picture of you two for old-time's sake. And if that doesn't work, I'll just snap a photo and run." She grinned. "Good thing I'm wearing flats today."

They were only a few miles from Estelle's estate when they pulled up in front of Garrison's estate. He lived in one of the older ranch houses on the edge of town. The house looked as though it had fallen on hard times as some homes do when the owner grows older and weary. Estelle had said Wyatt was a widower, which might explain it.

Estelle took the lead up the walk and used the large brass horseshoe-shaped knocker to announce their arrival. She started to knock a second time when the door opened.

Indeed, the gentleman who opened the door appeared older with graying hair and of medium height and build.

Deena immediately recognized him as one of the men she had seen arguing near the coin collection at the auction.

"Estelle Fitzhugh," the man said. "I never expected to see you here at my door. To what do I owe the pleasure? Although, I think I can guess."

"Nice to see you *Unc*—I mean, Wyatt. This is my sister-in-law, Deena Sharpe. May we come in?"

He nodded and stepped back. The large room, dark but clean, had over-stuffed furniture and heavy drapes.

"I just wanted to check on you," Estelle said. "I've heard a dreadful rumor that I was sure couldn't possibly have been the truth."

She sounded just like her mother. Like a chameleon, Estelle had slipped back into her upper-crustiness.

"Please, have a seat. May I get you a drink? Hot tea, perhaps."

"No, but thank you for your kindness." Estelle folded her hands in her lap and crossed her ankles.

Deena tried sitting up straighter than usual, but the deep leather chair made it a challenge.

Wyatt put his hand on his chin in professorial pose. "I suppose you've caught wind of my possible involvement in the theft of your father's coin collection. Let me assure you that I did not take the coins. In fact, I am rather distraught that they are missing. You know how much I admired your father's collection."

Estelle raised an eyebrow. "Actually, I know nothing about that."

"Why, I'm sure your mother must have mentioned it." He seemed genuinely surprised by her comment.

Estelle squared her shoulders and lifted her chin. "My mother was not one to gossip. Please explain what you mean."

"Estelle, dear, you know how much I cared for your father...and you. You were such a playful little thing. Anyway, when your father passed away, I offered to buy his entire coin collection from your mother, but she would hear none of it."

"Mother was quite protective of Father's family history."

"History is precisely why I wanted those coins. You may not know it, but some of those coins date back to the Civil War, the Revolution, and even earlier."

Estelle appeared unmoved.

"The real prize, however, are the silver dollars struck with the faces of Sam Houston and Stephen F. Austin from the Republic of Texas. They were never circulated, and your father's collection contains the only known examples. They're priceless."

Estelle looked as surprised as Deena felt. It didn't take a numismatist to understand the significance of those coins.

"I had no idea." She shook her head. "Did Mother know?"

"I tried to explain to her that those rare coins belonged in a museum, not in a private collection. She seemed to think I was trying to rob her like some common horse thief. Anyway, she threw me out, and from that day forward she would never speak to me again."

It sure seemed to Deena like he had a motive to take the coins. This new revelation actually made Wyatt Garrison appear even more guilty, not less. "Mr. Garrison, were those Texas coins in the collection at the auction on Saturday?"

He shook his head. "Luckily, they were not. I sincerely hope they are still in your possession, Estelle. Are they locked in a safe?"

"I—I took the rest of Father's collection to the bank for safe keeping. I would assume they are in there."

Good girl. Estelle had made it clear the coins were not at the house.

"And what do you plan to do with them?"

It seemed like a pushy question under the circumstances. Did it really matter at this point?

Estelle grimaced. "I have no plans. For now, I just need to know who stole the other collection. That person killed Leonard Dietz, you know."

Wyatt covered his mouth with his hand. "No, I didn't realize that. The newspaper said his death was under investigation. I assumed it was an accident."

"Mr. Garrison, did you know Leonard Dietz?" Deena asked.

"Ahh, Leonard. I remember him well. A fine gentleman. Always cordial and professional."

"So, you knew Leonard," Deena said. "Is that right?"

"Of course. This is a small town and most of the people in our circle knew each other's help."

"Did you happen to speak to him the night of the auction?" Deena leaned forward.

"No, no. I never saw him until...after."

"And have you been to Estelle's house in the last month or so?"

He narrowed his eyes. "What? Of course not."

Estelle stood up. "Wyatt, I need to know the truth. Did you take those coins? Maybe you did and then hit Leonard by accident. Deena knows an excellent defense attorney. If it was an accident—"

"That's quite enough, my dear. I have told you the truth, and that's the end of it. You know I am not that sort of person, even if your mother didn't." He stood up too, a signal for them to leave.

Deena pulled the phone from her handbag. "How about a picture for old-time's sake."

Estelle tilted her head and took hold of his arm. Her tone softened. "Oh yes, please...Uncle Wyatt."

One again, Estelle had changed her stripes. First a tiger, now a pussycat.

"Well, who could resist that." Wyatt struck a stately pose.

Zooming the camera in on his face, Deena snapped several pictures.

All they really needed was one good shot for the photo lineup. It might be the key to either clearing a kindly old man or convicting him as a liar and sending him away to prison for all the rest of his days.

* * *

ESTELLE FIDDLED WITH her seat belt, ready to leap out of the car. She didn't even ask Deena where they were going. "Wyatt seemed utterly truthful. I think it's pretty clear that Ronnie is the thief, don't you? I can't wait to find out if he did it on his own or if others were involved."

"Ronnie did act guilty, that's for sure. But I want to wait to see what Abby has to say before I make up my mind."

"I'll call her to see if she's home."

Luck was on their side. Estelle called and Abby was at home. Estelle told her to stay put and that they were on their way over.

When Estelle hung up, Deena frowned and said, "We can't go over there just yet. We only have two pictures. It won't be much of a photo lineup with just two people in it."

"So what are we going to do?"

Deena pulled into a church parking lot so she could think. "In a police lineup, they get other officers to participate or pull someone out of the drunk tank to step in. What we need is a place where we can find a couple of old guys hanging out in the middle of the afternoon. Any ideas?"

"The park?"

"*Eww.* No." Deena pictured dirty old men watching children play on swing sets. "I don't want photos of stalkers."

"Well then, what do you suggest?"

She narrowed her eyes. "Where would people like Russell and Cliff go?" Then it hit her. "I know. The VFW. They go there sometimes when they are in town."

"Excellent idea." Estelle clapped her hands together like a child.

The VFW building sat catty-corner to the fire station. Deena pulled up and parked. "If all else fails, maybe we can get pictures of some hot firemen." She winked at Estelle.

A couple of guys sat smoking on a bench on the side of the building. Too young, Deena thought.

She and Estelle went inside. Several men stood around a pool table while another few sat on stools at the food counter. The place smelled like stale cigarettes and old cooking oil.

"Hello, ladies. Is there something we can help you with?" The fellow who spoke appeared to be in his early sixties. His gray beard and long hair made him look like a roadie for Willie Nelson.

"Hi. I'm Deena and this is Estelle."

"Nice to meet you. I'm George." He tipped his ball cap.

Russell had a similar one showing his service in Vietnam, Deena noted.

"We are doing a photo story on people who live in small towns in Texas and were hoping to take a few pictures." Sometimes it was scary how well she could lie.

Estelle looked at her with a mixture of surprise and admiration.

"I see." He cocked his head. "Where's your camera?"

"Here." Deena pulled out her cell phone.

"That don't look like no camera a professional photographer would use."

"Oh, we're not professionals. In fact—" She turned to Estelle, looking for backup.

Her face said she didn't have any.

Deena scratched her nose. "In fact, we are amateurs taking a class at the community college."

"What kind of class?" He lifted his cap and scratched his head.

"Sociology." Deena gave him her warmest smile. "We don't even need your names—just your pictures. Since veterans are local heroes, we thought this would be a great place to come."

He nodded and grinned. "Well, since you put it that way, I guess there'd be no harm."

George raised his glass of soda and posed while she snapped pictures. Then he introduced them to the pool players, and she got pictures of them.

Before they left, George insisted on a selfie with the two women. They couldn't very well refuse.

On their way out the door, George patted Deena's rump.

She flinched. He was lucky he didn't get a karate kick to the throat—or the knee.

Actually, who was she kidding? She couldn't get her leg that high if she tried. Instead, she shot him a look , knowing it probably didn't even faze the old cuss.

George. Deena wanted to remember his name so she could tell her brother to give him a good talking-to about how to treat women. Certainly, she would never be coming back there.

They got back in the car and headed for Abby's apartment.

Estelle scrolled through the pictures on the phone. "I can't believe how easily those lies flowed out of your mouth."

"I know. I'm not proud of it, but it does come in handy sometimes. Remember, I taught high school kids for more than thirty years—I learned from the best."

"Ha," Estelle said. "I'll let you do the talking. I'll try not to put my foot in my mouth this time."

Deena had heard that before. Would Estelle actually be able to do it this time?

They pulled up to the complex and found the apartment. No wreath hung from the door, no plants decorated the stoop. Nothing indicated who might live inside.

Abby opened the door before they even knocked and stepped outside. She must have been hoping to make it a short visit.

Deena took out her phone. "We'd like you to look at some pictures to see if you recognize any of these people as the man you let into the house."

Abby folded her arms. Her yoga pants and hoodie offered little resistance to the cold November wind. "Okay, but it was a long time ago, so I may not remember."

"That's fine, just do your best." Deena scrolled to the picture of Ronnie Clark and handed her the phone.

She pulled it closer to her face and handed it back, shaking her head.

"Here's the next one."

She took the phone. "That's him! I remember now. That's the guy." Her eyes were wide with excitement.

Deena held up her hand. "Oh, I forgot to tell you to wait until you have seen all five pictures to say anything."

"I don't have to see any more. That's the guy. I'm positive."

Estelle grabbed the phone and gasped at the picture of Wyatt Garrison.

Although Abby seemed certain, Deena wanted to make it more legitimate. She took the phone and went through the motions of showing the girl the last three pictures.

"Like I said, that second one was the guy. I remember now that he looked a little like this man on one of the soaps I watch."

"Aren't you too young for soap operas?" Deena asked.

"I clean houses. The women I work for almost always have them on."

Estelle nodded in agreement. "Abby, this man is a friend of mine."

"See! I told you so. That's what he told me." She stuck her chin out.

"Still, I can't imagine you would just let him roam the house unsupervised. Surely you watched him when he left. Did he take anything with him?"

She lowered her eyes. "I guess I might as well tell you since you'll probably find out anyway. You see, he said it was urgent that he get the book he needed. When I said I couldn't let him in, he offered me money."

Estelle took a step back. "He bribed you?"

She nodded. All defiance had disappeared. "Yes, ma'am. He gave me a hundred-dollar bill and said it would be our secret. I know that was wrong," she quickly added, "but a hundred dollars is a lot of money. I'm trying to save up so I can move away from here and get a good, decent job."

"There is no shame in cleaning houses, my dear," Estelle said, reverting back to her mother's tone.

"That's not my only job." Abby shifted her weight back and forth, either from nerves or the cold wind. "I'm also a dancer. And not the kind you would see at one of your fancy theaters."

"Oh, I see." Estelle looked away this time. "You never told me that."

"I try to keep it quiet. You know how all those Bluebonnet Club ladies would react if they found out. 'Don't let the door hit you on your way out.' That's what they'd say."

Abby had a point. Deena wanted to know more. "I saw you the other day at Billy Ratliff's place. You looked pretty cozy with Leroy Johnson. How do you know him?"

"We all know each other from high school. He's just a friend." She pulled the hoodie tighter around her. "Look, it's cold. Are we done?"

"I have one more question," Deena said. "Where were you Saturday night during the auction?"

"Like I told that detective, I was at work at the club. The Boots and Babes on the highway. You can ask. They'll back me up."

"I've heard of it." Deena made a mental note.

Abby turned to Estelle. Her eyes grew misty. "Are you going to tell everyone about my other job? If so, I just know they'll all fire me."

"No, my dear." Estelle patted Abby's arm. "And I expect you at nine o'clock sharp tomorrow morning. Mr. Sinclair has been asking for your pork ribs."

Abby's face exploded into a smile, and she disappeared back into her apartment.

"Maybe we misjudged Ronnie Clark," Deena said as they got back into the car. "Maybe his outburst was just his bad temper rearing its ugly head."

"Maybe," Estelle said. She rubbed her temple with the tips of her fingers. "I don't want to think that Wyatt Garrison is a liar and a thief."

"And a killer."

Estelle turned and leaned her head back as she stared out at the road.

It's hard when you feel betrayed by someone you thought you could trust. Deena could relate. She reached over and patted Estelle's arm. Unfortunately, things would probably get tougher before they got better.

* * *

WHEN THEY RETURNED to the house, Russell was out back working on a project. He seemed surprised to see them. "Aren't you two supposed to be at the thrift shop? Did something happen?"

Estelle stayed outside to fill Russell in on their latest exploits while Deena went in the house. She found a pitcher of sweet tea and sat down at the old oak table in the kitchen. It reminded her of the farm table her grandmother used to have. The one she sat at when she would cut up vegetables for stew and roll her dough for fresh bread. Deena wondered if Russell, being a few years older, had the same memories when he sat in this room.

Deena needed paper. She could always think better when she doodled notes. The back staircase beckoned her. She climbed the stairs to the study to find paper and a pen. The room gave her a bit of the creeps as she looked around. After all, it was the very same room where Russell and Estelle almost died last spring.

Deena hurried over to the desk and pulled out a few pieces of stationery and a pen. Something seemed odd, as if she wasn't alone. Was someone watching her? Not wanting to wait around for any paranormal experiences, she shut the door behind her.

A sound, not quite animal and not quite human, startled her. She looked down to see Clover the cat, back arched, ready to attack. Deena apologized and stepped around her, then raced back down to the kitchen. Her heart pounded out of her chest as she sat back down at the table. Her imagination must have been working overtime.

Using the supplies she had retrieved, Deena made her usual chart of suspects with columns for motive and opportunity. She wrote Abby's name first. Clearly, if she had been involved in the plot, her motive would be money. Deena wrote a dollar sign on the paper. Opportunity? If she had wanted to steal something, she could have done it anytime while she was here alone. She wouldn't need to invent a wild story about a stranger coming to the house. Besides, Estelle hadn't found anything missing from the house. It would be easy enough to check out Abby's alibi. In fact, Guttman had probably already made it around to the Boots and Babes Club to check it out. She crossed Abby's name off the list.

Billy, Leroy, Ronnie Clark, and finally, Wyatt Garrison, were the other names she added to the list. Deena didn't want to think that an actual acquaintance of Estelle's could be the culprit, but it was beginning to look that way. *Motive?* Obviously, Wyatt would have been looking for the coins when he bribed Abby to let him look around the house. When he didn't find them, he would have left empty-handed.

Besides that, Wyatt was probably the only suspect who knew Leonard personally. That would explain why Corey said he had seen them talking outside of the car. How or why that conversation turned deadly was still a mystery.

Estelle and Russell came in through the back door.

Estelle wiped her feet. "Iced tea?" She shivered as she looked at Deena's glass. "I'll put on a pot of coffee."

"Sis, are you okay?" Russell hung up his coat on a hook near the door.

"Of course. Why wouldn't I be?"

"According to Estelle, you may have caught a killer today."

Deena looked back toward the kitchen. "Is that what you think, Estelle? That Wyatt is the killer?"

Estelle kept her back to them. "As much as I hate to believe it, it's the only logical conclusion. He admitted to wanting the coins for years. And now we know he had come looking for them. I wonder why he didn't just ask me for them?" She turned around. Her face had lost its color.

"Here, let me make the coffee." Russell led Estelle to the table.

Deena smiled proudly at her brother. After being single for sixty-something years, he had truly embraced married life.

He must have guessed her thoughts based on the smile she gave him. "See? I can be chivalrous." He opened the cabinet to pull out the cups.

Estelle leaned over, checking out Deena's notes. "What's that?"

"A list of suspects and their motives. I hope it's okay that I got some stationery from your mother's desk."

"That's fine. What have you come up with?"

"I think we can eliminate Billy, Abby, and Leroy as suspects. I don't think any of them were involved. If they were part of some master scheme, I doubt they would be hanging out smoking dope as though nothing had happened. Guilty people are rarely that calm and collected. They make mistakes by either doing something or saying something out of the ordinary."

Estelle nodded. "That's why I'm so perplexed by Wyatt. He didn't seem like he was hiding anything."

"Although," Deena reminded her, "he didn't seem all that surprised to see you."

"That's true."

The coffee pot chugged in the kitchen as the aroma of fresh roasted beans wafted across the room.

"Still making coffee the old-fashioned way, I see," Deena said.

"It's still the best way." Russell brought the cups over on a tray and sat down. "So what now? Are you going to call the police and tell them about this Wyatt Garrison fella?"

Estelle's sickly appearance had worsened. "I suppose we don't have much choice."

"I wish I could say that I trusted Detective Guttman to do the right thing," Deena said. "It seems political pressure makes him quick to pull the trigger and make an arrest before all the facts are in. But, he's all we've got."

As she pulled out her phone, she said a little silent prayer, hoping she was doing the right thing. She took a deep breath when he answered. "Detective Guttman, could you come over to the Fitzhugh house? We have something important to tell you."

Chapter 12

THE LITTLE NEIGHBORHOOD in Butterfly Gardens always offered a welcome respite for Deena after a long day of antiquing or shopping or sleuthing. Although she knew secrets were hiding behind every brightly painted, wreath-covered door, she chose to view the area as a safe haven, free of turmoil and tragedy.

Boy, was she wrong.

Before she could even get out of her car, Gary was standing by her door bursting with the latest news.

"You'll never guess what happened. I mean, not in a million years." He clasped his hands.

Deena wasn't in the mood for games. "Okay, then just tell me."

"Christy Ann got cited by the police for disturbing the peace. They nearly threw her in the pokey for assault from what I heard."

"You're kidding!" Deena stood with her mouth open staring at the house across the street. Normally, the blinds would be open, but now the place looked closed up like Fort Knox.

Gary seemed to take delight in being the one with neighborhood gossip for a change. "And you'll never guess what it was about."

"Don't tell me. Cookies?"

His face fell. "How'd you know?"

She pointed to the back seat.

"Oh, I see she got to you, too," he said. "Let's go inside and I'll tell you all about it."

"Sounds good. And I'll tell you all about finding the thief who stole the Fitzhugh coin collection."

"What?" Gary stopped and held the front door open.

"Yep. And you'll never guess how."

"How?"

"Well, it all started with cookies."

* * *

HURLEY DANCED AROUND, happy to see her, as usual, so she flipped him a cookie out of one of the boxes. The saga of the neighborhood drama lifted her spirits. "Maybe I should walk over and check on Christy Ann, just to see how she's doing, of course."

Gary grinned. "Just to be nosy, you mean."

"Okay, I admit it. I want to know exactly what happened. Maybe I can drop a couple of snarky remarks. It's not like I don't owe her any."

"Suit yourself. I'll fire up the grill for burgers."

Deena headed across the street and knocked on the door. When no one answered, she rang the bell. If the baby was asleep, she'd have to answer the door to shut Deena up. Sure enough, on the second ring, Parker, Christy Ann's husband, answered the door.

"Hey, Deena," he said. "Christy Ann is lying down. She has a headache. Can I do something for you?"

"Sounds like she's not the only one with a headache, from what I hear." *Ooh. Such a good line. Wish I could have said it to her face.*

"Is that Deena?" Christy Ann whispered from behind the door. "Get in here quick."

She obeyed and Parker headed off to the den to tend to the screeching kids. Maybe they were only laughing, but to Deena, it sounded like a ruckus.

"What did you hear?" Christy Ann seemed to have been bingeing on one of the boxes of Peanut Butter Delights. Crumbs covered her blouse. She offered one to Deena.

"No thanks. I have plenty, remember?"

"So tell me what you heard."

"Gary said you got cited for disturbing the peace. He also mentioned something about assault."

She paced across the foyer and then sat on the sofa in the formal living room. Deena followed her lead. "That Sarah Garrett. Thinks she knows everything. Tried to say I cheated in the cookie sale."

"Cheated? What do you mean? Were you using steroids or something?"

An exasperated gasp escaped from Christy Ann's lips. "Since you don't have kids, you don't know what it's like to go up to a stranger's door and try to sell them stuff. It's not fun, I can tell you."

Oh, you might be surprised.

"Anyway, she's the chairman of the Pee Wee League—that's another whole story. She divided the neighborhood into territories. You can only go door-to-door in your assigned area."

"Uh-oh. Did you invade someone else's territory?"

"Not exactly. Little Davey and I were just going for a stroll to the playground. He was in the wagon and there just happened to be some of the cookie boxes inside."

"Of course."

"I mean, he might have needed a snack, you know. I couldn't help it if some people saw us and asked to buy cookies. It would give the league a bad reputation to turn away patrons, right?"

Deena clinched her teeth to avoid saying what she really thought. After all, Christy Ann had been through a lot already. No use kicking her when she was down.

"When some of the other moms found out, they sent that awful Sarah woman over here to chew me out. If you ask me, she's just jealous because her child doesn't play sports as well as Davey."

"So you assaulted her."

From the other room, Deena heard Parker yell at the children to hold their voices down so he could read the newspaper.

"Deena! You know I'm a pacifist. I can't help it that a box of cookies slipped out of my hand and hit the back of her head accidently."

"Accidently hit the back of her head?"

"There were no witnesses, and I'm sticking to my story."

Parker stuck his head in the room. "Honey, can you watch the kids so I can go pick us up something for supper?"

Christy Ann looked annoyed but nodded.

"What? You're not cooking?" Deena teased.

Christy Ann tilted her head. "Come on now. You know the kind of day I've had. You must feel like this all the time, you poor thing."

She searched for a snappy comeback but came up dry.

"Listen, Deena, you're one of my best friends."

I am? It was news to her.

"Do what you can to help smooth things over if you hear any malicious gossip about me. Also, I'm going to be volunteering for the Bluebonnet Club with a service project on Saturday. Maybe you could come and say sweet things about me."

"But the Bluebonnet Club is a bunch of older ladies. I thought you were in the Junior League."

"I am, but that doesn't stop me from helping the less fortunate whenever I can. See? I'm a really special person."

"You're special, that's for sure."

Christy Ann smiled sweetly. "Some of my friends have aunts and grandmothers in the Bluebonnet Club. The older women can spread the word about how selfless I am for helping out. So will you come? It's for a good cause."

"I'll check my calendar," Deena said and headed to the door. "Stay out of trouble, you hear? Oh, and you might want to go easy on those cookies. I think you may have put on a few pounds."

She didn't stop to look at Christy Ann's expression. Luckily, Deena got out the door without a box of cookies slamming into the back of her head.

Chapter 13

THERE'S NOTHING quite like being awoken in the middle of the night by a phone call from the police. Your mind jumps to all kinds of horrible conclusions.

When she heard the word *police* on the other end of the line, Deena immediately pictured her parents living out their golden years in Hawaii. Had something happened? A boating accident perhaps, or a shark attack? She pictured that poor girl in the opening scene of *Jaws*.

It took a minute for her pulse rate to lower after she hung up.

"Who was it?" Gary grumbled when she turned on the table lamp.

"The police."

He shot up in bed. "What is it? Is it Mother?"

"No, it's nothing like that. There's been a break-in at the thrift shop, and they need me to come down there." She threw back the covers.

Gary let out a sigh of relief. "I'm coming with you. I don't want you out alone this time of night."

The small shopping center housing the thrift shop looked like the midway at a carnival with all the flashing lights out front. Deena counted three police cruisers in the parking lot. Imagine her surprise when she went inside to find the police with four grown adults in custody. It was like stumbling upon the Watergate burglars.

Russell, Estelle, Penelope, and her husband, Edwin, all sat in folding chairs with their hands cuffed behind their backs.

"What on earth is going on?" Deena stood in the doorway of the storeroom. An odd burnt smell attacked her nostrils.

Officer Hitchcock—apparently the busiest man on the force—took the lead. "Ma'am, one of our officers saw cars and lights on in the place, which is highly unusual for this time of night. Upon further investigation, we found these unauthorized persons inside. They may have been trying to commit arson."

Russell started to stand, but the officer guarding him pushed him back down into the chair. "That's ridiculous," Russell said. "I tried to explain, but they—"

"Pipe down. You'll get your chance," Hitchcock demanded.

"Officer, this is my brother and these are my...friends." Deena wasn't sure if she should be horrified or amused.

"Did you authorize them to be in here tonight?"

"No. I mean, it's okay, I guess."

"Are you answering under your own free will or do they have something on you?"

Gary held out his hands. "Officer, there's obviously been a mistake. Can you please remove their handcuffs? I'm sure there's a reasonable explanation for all this." He looked at Russell and Estelle. "Right?"

"You bet your booty, there is!" Penelope screeched. "Wait till I get out of here. Wait till I get my lawyer!" She wriggled her hands behind her back.

Hitchcock pointed his nightstick at her. "This one's the reason for the handcuffs. She tried to bite one of our officers."

Deena snorted out a chuckle.

Estelle shot her a look that said she wasn't the least bit amused.

"Officer Hitchcock," Deena said sweetly, turning on the charm, "you remember Ms. Fitzhugh from the auction, right? She's just been through a terrible ordeal."

"Fitzhugh? You said the name was Sinclair." He reached for his notepad. "I even wrote it down."

"That's right," Estelle said through clenched teeth. "Estelle Fitzhugh Sinclair. If you had just let us explain..."

"Un-cuff them immediately," he shouted to the other officers. "These fine people have done nothing wrong." His face had turned blotchy red with a hint of green around the gills. "I apologize for bringing you all the way down here."

"Thank you, officer," Deena said. "And thank you *all* for keeping Maycroft safe from ne'er-do-wells and other criminal elements." She stifled a grin.

Hitchcock tipped his hat. "We'll just be getting out of your way now, ma'am. Let's go, fellas." They were out the door in a hurry.

The four would-be convicts stood up and started gathering their things.

"Not so fast," Deena said sternly, like a concerned mother to her children. "Someone needs to tell me what's going on here."

Penelope started to speak, but Estelle held up her hand. "Let me. It was my idea. Why don't you and Edwin get back home. I'll speak to you tomorrow."

"Fine with me," Penelope said. "I could use a hot toddy after this." She and her husband left the shop.

Estelle pointed to a chair.

"That's okay," Deena said. "I'll stand. By the way, how did y'all get in here? I have the keys."

Estelle took a seat and sighed. "Russell picked the lock."

Deena shook her head. Her brother had many hidden talents, not all of them good.

Estelle folded her hands in her lap. True confession time. "I called Penelope to ask for her help."

"Help with what? Pricing clothes in the middle of the night?"

"Come on, Deena. You know what people say about her. She has certain...*powers*. I thought they might be useful."

"I have no idea what you're talking about. What powers?"

"Everyone says she's a witch."

"A witch?" Deena almost fell backwards. She sat down next to Estelle.

"That's right."

Deena shook her head, thinking she had heard wrong. "Are you sure you're not confusing that with a different word that rhymes with 'witch'?"

"No, silly. I called her because I was hoping she could tell us about the signs. I tried my best to connect them to Wyatt Garrison, but I kept coming up empty. I thought Penelope might be able to contact Mother and—"

"Don't tell me she has a crystal ball or was mixing up a magic soup. Is that what that awful smell is coming from?"

"No. It's burnt hair. We were having a séance."

Just when you think you've heard it all, you find out something even more incredible. Deena couldn't fathom that her brother had agreed to participate in a hokey ceremony to contact his wife's dead mother in order to find out how some random happenings at a store were connected to the death of his wife's chauffeur. Sure, he believed in UFOs and every conspiracy theory ever floated, but this? Things certainly couldn't get any weirder.

Chapter 14

STRONG COFFEE from the doughnut shop served by a twenty-something yuppie with a man-bun barely kept Deena awake on her way to work Wednesday morning. She would be better off with toothpicks propping open her eyelids after the restless night she'd had.

There was a time when she could stay up all night studying for a test or grading papers and still appear fresh as a daisy the next day. Not anymore. She felt more like rancid old meat.

Hoping for a quiet day at the thrift shop, she looked through the new donations that had been left at the back door. Not surprisingly, there were lots of summer clothes. This time of year in the South, people cleaned out their closets to make way for their winter duds.

She sorted through the items, separating the ones that could be resold from the ones with holes and tears. Unfortunately, some people donate anything, regardless of the condition. *Seriously? Old underpants?* Many of the items would be headed to the recycling center.

Estelle had said she might not be in today. A day without ghosts and signs and drama would be a welcome relief.

A few of the regulars stopped by to visit and search for vintage treasures. It was shaping up to be a peaceful day. Deena started to call Sandra to check on her and the baby when the jingle of the door brought her back to reality.

It was Estelle and she was in a state.

"Russell just dropped me off. You'll never guess what happened."

This sounded like a conversation Deena wasn't prepared to have. She reached for her now-cold coffee.

"Detective Guttman called me to let me know they have just arrested Wyatt Garrison."

"Already? How on earth—"

"Not on murder charges, but on attempted robbery. Guttman went over to talk to him yesterday afternoon since we said Abby had identified him. Wyatt confessed to going over to the house to try to find the coins. They took him in a little while ago."

"Wow. So does Guttman think he's the killer?"

"He wouldn't really say. He just thought I would want to know about the arrest."

"I know how this works." Deena said and went to refill her cup. "Guttman's probably arrested Wyatt on robbery charges so he can make sure he doesn't run off while they gather evidence for the homicide case."

"But what about Ronnie Clark? Are we positive he's not guilty?"

"I wish I could talk to Guttman to find out what evidence he has, but I know he won't talk to me again. Even after telling him about our findings yesterday, he seemed annoyed and told me to stay out of his way."

"After all we did for him..."

Deena blew on the hot brew. "What do you think? You know Wyatt Garrison better than the rest of us. Do you think he could actually be guilty of stealing the coins from the auction?"

"That's the thing," Estelle said. "I just don't know. Russell says people can change based on their circumstances and that maybe something made Wyatt desperate for the coins."

"Desperate enough to kill someone he knew?"

Estelle shook her head and slumped down in a chair. "I find it so hard to believe. That's why I need a favor from you."

Deena bristled. "What?"

"Can you go to the police station with me to talk to him?"

"Talk to who, Guttman?"

"No, Wyatt. You've been there before, so you know the ropes."

"Hmm. Do you know if he has an attorney yet? That may make a difference."

"I have no clue."

Deena looked around the shop. "We'll need to wait a while until he's booked, then I guess we can head over there. I can't promise you they'll let us see him. He might refuse, you know."

"I'm willing to take that chance. I want to look him in the eyes when I ask him if he killed Leonard." She blew out a breath. "It comes in handy to have a private investigator in the family."

"Semi-private. I work for Sandra's husband, remember? By the way, if Ian is representing Wyatt, that may complicate matters. I really doubt he is. Wyatt probably has one of those pricey defense attorneys from Lyon and Sons."

Estelle pulled off her jacket. "I'm just going to check in the storage closet while we wait. Maybe I'll get another sign."

"Surely you're kidding."

"Not at all. At this point, I assume we need all the help we can get."

Deena creased her brow. "Yes, but from the living, not the dead."

Chapter 15

THE FRONT DESK SERGEANT at the police station said he would have to check to see if Wyatt Garrison could have visitors yet. He asked if Deena wanted to speak to Detective Guttman. She tried not to sound too suspicious when she gave him a resounding no.

Estelle flipped through pages of a sports magazine while they waited. Deena searched the internet on her phone for Wyatt Garrison's name, wondering if word was out yet that he'd been arrested. Dan at the newspaper would probably be covering the story.

The officer came out and spoke to them. "Mr. Garrison wants to speak to you. Follow me back to the visitation room."

It was just as Deena remembered it. Cold and stark with small glass-enclosed carrels and vinyl chairs for visitors. They sat at the first window and waited.

"This is just like on TV," Estelle whispered, trembling with anticipation.

"Why are you whispering?" Deena asked.

Estelle pointed to a sign warning visitors that their conversations were being monitored.

"That's for conversations on the phone, not out here."

After several minutes, Wyatt Garrison, wearing handcuffs and escorted by a uniformed guard, shuffled to the window and sat down. He looked to have aged a few years since yesterday. Orange was definitely not his color. Estelle picked up the receiver and held it so that Deena could listen, too.

Wyatt spoke first. "I'm glad you came. Surely you believe me when I say I didn't steal those coins."

"I'm not sure what to believe," Estelle said. "After all, you confessed to bribing my housekeeper and trying to steal them from my home. What on earth possessed you to do that?"

"I was afraid you were going to sell them. When I heard about the auction, I was worried they'd end up in the hands of some city slicker from up North, or even worse, in another country. I told you, those coins belong in a museum here in Texas."

"Sounds to me like you wanted them so badly that you stole them during the auction. Then Leonard caught you, so you knocked him down and killed him."

"No! As I told you, the collection in the auction did not include the rare Texas coins. Sure, I was prepared to bid on the others, but I didn't want that set enough to steal them."

Estelle shook her head and looked at Deena, then put her ear back to the receiver. "So you admit you would have stolen them from my house if you had found them. If you had wanted them that badly, why didn't you just ask me for them?"

Beads of sweat formed on his forehead. "I thought about it, believe me. In fact, that's why I came to your house in the first place. Then when your housekeeper said you were out of town, I decided to just take a look in the study. Your father used to keep them on a small library table. And yes, I bribed the girl to let me go upstairs. I hope you don't blame her. After all, I have a very innocent face." He offered up a faint smile.

Deena didn't want the old guy trying to charm Estelle. "Mr. Garrison, when you didn't find the collection in the study, what did you do next?"

The smile disappeared. He wiped his forehead against his arm. "I walked out into the hall and checked some of the doors. When I opened the door across from the large bedroom, I saw what appeared to be a storage room. I looked through the items but didn't find the coins. In fact, I gave up quickly, realizing I was treading on thin ice, legally speaking."

"But you were Father's friend. How could you even consider stealing one of his most prized possessions?"

"I know how it sounds, my dear, but I had every intention of returning them after the auction was over. I was going to make an appointment with your new husband, who I assume is a reasonable sort of fellow, and explain the importance of the collection. I assumed you would be *thanking* me, not pressing charges against me."

The explanation seemed flimsy to Deena. "And why would you wait until after the auction? Why not have this meeting beforehand?"

He narrowed his eyes at her. "Because, I knew if Estelle had turned out anything like her mother, she would be too emotional to have a rational conversation about anything having to do with her father during a time she was letting go of some of her family heirlooms. I thought it best to wait."

He had that right. In fact, everything he said made sense.

"Estelle, dear, you must believe me. I have no cause to steal from you. My motive for getting my hands on those coins has always been historic, not financial. I have plenty of money for myself, my children, and my grandchildren. I'm sure you know that."

Estelle pulled the phone back from Deena and nodded to give her some space.

Deena got up and went to the back of the room so Estelle could talk privately. She paced back and forth with her hands in the pockets of her jacket. If Wyatt was telling the truth, a thief was still at large. Perhaps they'd been correct to suspect Ronnie Clark after all.

A few minutes later, the guard returned and escorted Wyatt away.

Estelle remained seated.

"What is it?" Deena asked. "Are you all right?"

A tear slid down her cheek. "Deena, I think we've made a terrible mistake. Uncle Wyatt is innocent."

Deena didn't know what to say. They had opened a can of worms by telling Guttman about Wyatt Garrison, that was for sure. And putting the lid back on that can wasn't going to be easy.

* * *

ESTELLE SPOKE LITTLE on the way back to the house. She said she wasn't up to going back to the shop.

That was okay by Deena, although she did accept her invitation to have a sandwich before heading back. Something about this amateur police work made her hungry.

"Thank you, dear," Estelle said as Abby placed the sandwiches on the table.

Russell joined them for lunch and wanted to hear all about their visit to the jail. Estelle shushed him and cocked her head toward Abby, making it clear she didn't want to talk in front of the girl.

"That barbeque sauce smells delicious," Deena said. "You'll have to save me one of those pork ribs to try out."

"You wish." Russell made a stop sign with his hand. "Only thing better than those pork ribs are the *leftover* pork ribs." He winked at Abby.

"There you go hoggin' all the good stuff, just like when we were kids." Deena grabbed a pickle spear off of Russell's plate before he could stop her.

Abby's cell phone rang, and she ducked back into the kitchen.

"What happened?" Russell whispered. "Did Wyatt confess?"

"Not now," Estelle answered. "After lunch."

Abby returned, her face a ghostly white. She untied her apron. "I'm sorry, Mrs. Sinclair. I have to go." Her words came out with quick breaths. "Can you take care of the sauce? You need to marinate—"

Estelle stood up. "What's the matter? Has something happened?"

"That was the hospital. It's Billy. He's been in an accident. Someone ran his motorcycle off the road." She grabbed her purse from a cupboard.

"Don't worry about anything. Just go," Estelle said. "Call us if you need anything."

Abby headed out the front door.

"What about the ribs?" Russell asked.

"Oh fiddle-faddle." Estelle hurried into the kitchen. "I can finish these up."

Russell's face dropped. "There goes dinner."

Deena laid down her sandwich and went into the kitchen to check on Estelle. "Need some help?"

"Yes. I've never made ribs in my life. I think she puts them in the oven and then on the grill." She stirred the thick sauce.

"How about this. We'll pour the sauce on the meat and then refrigerate it. I'm sure Russell can grill them up later."

"I guess that will work." Estelle turned off the heat and moved the pan so it could cool.

Deena pulled the package of ribs out of the refrigerator. "Poor Billy. Two accidents in the same week." *Same week.* The package of ribs slipped from her hand and fell to the floor.

"What on earth?" Estelle stared at Deena, waiting for her to pick up the package.

She stood frozen. "Unless it wasn't an accident!"

"What do you mean?"

"Whoever stole those coins may think that Billy got a good look at them. The driver of that car may have been trying to get rid of his witness."

Estelle gasped. "But you said Billy didn't see who hit him in the parking lot."

"But the killer doesn't know that." Deena picked up the package of meat and slung it onto the counter. "This might be just the break we need."

"Slow down," Estelle said, following her to the back door. "Where are you going?"

"To the hospital. Don't you see? If the person who stole the coins tried to kill Billy, then we have another suspect to clear."

"Who?"
"Wyatt Garrison."

Chapter 16

THE MAYCROFT REGIONAL Hospital had become much too familiar to Deena. Between her clumsiness and various brushes with danger, she practically had her own suite in the emergency room. That's where she went to find Abby, hoping to talk to Billy. Maybe he could identify the driver of the car who tried to hit him. Or should she say, kill him?

The receptionist told her Billy had been taken in for surgery and that his friends were most likely in the main waiting room on the second floor. She, of course, knew right where to go. Sure enough, Abby and Leroy were there along with a woman Deena assumed to be Billy's mother.

"Mrs. Sharpe, you didn't have to come down here," Abby said, although she had a look of relief on her face.

"I wanted to check on Billy. How is he?" Deena sat across from the small group.

Leroy rubbed his forehead. "The doctor said he got lucky. He's got a broken leg and some broken ribs, a sprained wrist, and a lot of—what was that word?" He looked at Abby.

"Contusions," she said. "They're working on his leg now. He had multiple fractures."

The woman next to them eyed Deena up and down. "How is it you know my boy?"

"I met Billy a few days ago after the auction. Abby works for my sister-in-law."

"Oh, okay." She went back to her magazine.

Abby had a death grip on Leroy's hand.

"Can you tell me what happened?" Deena asked.

"We didn't get a chance to talk to him. The police officer told us that Billy said a car ran him off the road over there by the South Loop. He was on his way to work. What's scary is that Billy said the car did it on purpose. It wasn't an accident."

"Did he say if it was the same car that hit him in the parking lot at the auction?"

Leroy shook his head. "The guy didn't tell us anything like that. I doubt Billy would have mentioned it to the cops."

"Did the police officer, say anything else?"

"Nah. He said they would follow up after Billy gets conscious." Leroy sat back and adjusted his John Deere trucker cap. "Man, I hate sitting around like this."

That seemed ironic since "sitting around" seemed to be the trio's favorite pastime. "Did you get the name of the officer you spoke to? I want to ask him some questions."

Abby frowned. "We don't want Billy to get into any trouble." She glanced down at Momma who seemed oblivious to their entire conversation. "He's had enough run-ins with the law."

Deena leaned forward. "But if someone is trying to harm Billy, we need to find out who it is, right?"

Abby glanced at Leroy who shrugged his shoulders as if handing off the problem to her.

"Look," Deena said, "we know Billy didn't do anything wrong just like you didn't do anything wrong." It was a lie, of course, but Deena wanted to gain the girl's trust. "I don't want anyone else to get hurt over this stupid mess."

Her frown softened. "It was a guy named Hitchcock. Like Wild Bill Hitchcock."

Here we go again. "Thanks. I promise to try to protect Billy. I'll be back tomorrow to check on him."

Abby nodded then looked away.

Deena was now more convinced of Wyatt Garrison's innocence. How, though, was she going to convince Guttman since he wouldn't even talk to her about the case? Maybe she could go around him through Hitchcock. At this point, she had few options.

* * *

THEY SAY THE POLICE force is a brotherhood. There's a bond as strong as family among those who wear the uniform. Deena had hoped that wasn't the case between the rank-and-file officers in Maycroft and the number one detective.

Apparently, it was.

Hitchcock proved to be useless. He said Guttman had warned the officers in the department not to talk to her about the case. Although it was probably a violation of her civil rights, she didn't have the time or energy to fret about it now.

She sat in the car and rubbed her right foot. Even though she'd been wearing flats, her feet felt like she'd been walking on hot coals. She'd gotten spoiled by not being on her feet all day. It was a reminder of how soft she'd gotten since retiring. Sleeping late, coming and going as she pleased, dropping by Gary's office for a quick visit and surprise lunch now and then—these were all perks of not being on the clock anymore.

On the other hand, she'd actually grown stronger as a person. Chasing after bad guys—and gals—will do that to a person.

She debated going back to the thrift store for a few more hours of work. Her barking dogs told her she needed a break. And perhaps a nap. Instead, she headed over to Sandra's house. Not only would holding her new goddaughter do her some good, she could explain why the thrift store wasn't bringing in much money this week. The last thing she needed was her best friend thinking she'd had her hand in the cookie jar.

As she crossed the intersection of Maple and Main, a siren blared behind her. With a quick glance in the rearview mirror, she saw Guttman with one of those portable lights on top of his unmarked car. She pulled into the parking lot of the laundromat. Ronnie Clark's laundromat, to be exact.

Deena got out of her car and walked up to his window. "Can I see your license and registration, officer?"

"Very funny. Get in."

She got in the passenger seat of his car and put her hand to her mouth, pretending to smoke a cigarette. "What's the topic for tonight?"

"What?"

"Sorry. I was playing Deep Throat from *All the President's Men*."

"Not now." He pulled his sunglasses off and tossed them on the dashboard. "I heard you called one of my officers about the case. Is that true?"

"Yes. You don't think one of your men would lie to you, do you?"

Not the slightest hint of a grin.

"You have a short memory. I told you—"

"You said I couldn't talk to you about the case. You never mentioned that I couldn't talk to anyone in the entire police force. What if I was being assaulted, or worse, someone was trying to steal my dog? Am I allowed to call 9-1-1?"

"Look. Let's cut to the chase. I'll give you thirty seconds. Shoot."

Thirty seconds was barely long enough to recite her phone number and address, much less catch him up on her investigation. "Someone is trying to kill Billy Ratliff. He was run off the road today and is in the hospital. It was probably the same person who ran into him when they were fleeing from the auction. That's how he really hurt his arm, not in a motorcycle accident. The killer must think Billy can ID him. One thing's for sure, Wyatt Garrison didn't do it because you have him locked up. Garrison admitted to trying to take the coins from the house, but he says he didn't take them at the auction."

Guttman's face remained stoic. He looked out the front window, staring off into the distance.

She held her breath, waiting for the inevitable tongue-lashing.

"When did you talk to Garrison?"

"Earlier today at the jail. Estelle asked me to go with her."

"Then you know we have him on attempted robbery, not homicide."

"Right. And I know that it is just a ruse to keep an eye on him."

"Is Billy okay?"

"Are you asking as a human being who cares about his fellow man or as a cop?"

"Both."

"He's pretty banged up. They are doing surgery to repair his leg. We can talk to him when he's back in his room."

"*We* will do no such thing. *I* will talk to him. If he's anything like he was the other day, he was higher than a kite and just imagined someone was trying to kill him."

"Linus, you don't honestly think that, do you?"

"I'm sure they'll run a toxicology report on him. We'll have to wait to see what it says. He lied to me once about his arm, who's to say he's not lying again?"

"In the meantime, are you going to have them drop the charges against Wyatt?"

"Absolutely not." He hesitated, then added, "Not yet at least. Wasn't it you who called me yesterday to pick Garrison up? If you're so sure he's innocent, who do you think did it? And who will you think is guilty tomorrow?"

Deena could feel her face flush. "That's not fair."

Guttman turned in his seat to face her. "When you're an outside investigator, it's easy to jump to conclusions based on a handful of evidence. When you're in my position, you have to look at all the facts. Investigate thoroughly."

"But you wouldn't even have known about Billy or Garrison if it hadn't been for me."

"Who's to say I wouldn't have gotten the information myself — eventually?"

Yeah, when pigs fly. Luckily, she hadn't said it out loud. "In answer to your question, I think Ronnie Clark is guilty."

"Okay, based on what evidence?"

She hesitated, knowing she couldn't just say, *Because of the way he yelled at me.* "I don't have any proof yet, but I'm working on it."

"Once again, I'd just ask you to let me do my job. This doesn't involve you. You pay your taxes. Let me earn my salary."

Deena yanked open the door and got out. "Fine. But if anything happens to my sister-in-law, I'm blaming you!" She slammed the door shut and got back in her car.

The detective's words had stung. Was it her sense of responsibility to Estelle and Russell that kept driving her forward, or was it her pride?

Regardless, she needed time to sort it all out.

After a heaping helping of Detective Guttman, Deena was in no mood to play cootchie-coo with baby Sylvia. She headed home for a warm bath and a glass of wine. The clock on the dashboard shook its finger at her, saying it was too early for wine. She'd have to settle for hot chocolate.

Hopefully, there had been no new shenanigans in the neighborhood today. She wanted to avoid Christy Ann, although she would normally be picking up her oldest up from Mother's Day Out about now. Sure enough, there she was unpacking her three children from the car when Deena drove up.

The garbage can lay overturned by the curb. Why couldn't they just stand them up after emptying them? She hurried to the mailbox down by the curb. She could have waited, but she had plans to slip into her jammies as soon as she got in the house.

When she pulled out the small stack of envelopes, something clattered to the ground.

"What's that?" Christy Ann asked from behind her. "Did you win the lottery or something?"

That woman was like a ninja. She could sneak up on you quicker than the women who spray perfume on you at the department stores.

Deena looked down on the ground to see something shiny. It was a coin. She turned it over in her hand, judging it to be a silver dollar.

"Looks like you got a gift," Christy Ann said.

Deena looked at a small envelope. The flap lay open and the outside was written, *Back off*. "Actually, it's more like a warning. And not a subtle one at that."

"A warning? What do you mean?"

Deena had no intention of telling Christy Ann about the coins and the murder and all the rest. "Oh, it's nothing," she said. "Just a little joke between Gary and me."

Christy Ann turned back toward her house.

"By the way," Deena called after her, "did you see anyone over here at my house today?"

She turned around and put her hands on her hips. "Are you implying I've been spying on your house?"

"No, of course not. But as the captain of the neighborhood watch—"

"Well, if you must know, Sarah Garrett and her sister purposely walked by the house with their kids in strollers. I think they were trying to get a reaction out of me. I wouldn't give them the satisfaction."

"Anyone else?"

"A few cars and an old truck. Probably one of those junk men who come around on garbage day."

"I see."

"If you want to know if your husband came home for lunch and had a tête-à-tête with another woman, the answer is no."

"My heavens! I would never suspect Gary of that."

"Neither would most of the women around here, but that doesn't mean they'd be right. Of course, that's none of my business."

Deena hurried into the house, clutching the coin. She closed the door and leaned back against it. Taking a deep breath she said, "See, Linus? It just got personal."

Chapter 17

DEENA ONLY KNEW of three people who could tell her if the coin she found in the mailbox was part of the stolen loot. One of those men was locked up, one was probably the thief, and one of them hated her guts. Unfortunately, number three was her best bet.

Her hot bath and chilled wine would have to wait. She drove over to the pawn shop to talk to Marty Fisk, hoping to convince him that Guttman needed her help solving this case. She would take her best shot. If nothing else, she might be able to get a lead on the coin and its sender.

Only two cars were parked in front of the store. Fisk would have a hard time avoiding her in a nearly empty shop. She dropped the coin in her purse and went inside. A guy with greasy hair and a neck tattoo had his feet propped up on a chair. His eyes were closed and his mouth hung open like a fly-trap. He appeared to be the only one in the shop.

Deena tapped on the glass countertop.

The young man fell backwards then popped up when he saw her.

"Whew," he said, wiping the back of his hand across his forehead dramatically. "I thought you were the boss for a second there."

"I take it Mr. Fisk isn't in."

"Nope. Uh, you're not going to tell him I was asleep on the job, are you?"

She shook her head. "Do you know when he'll be back?"

He glanced at the clock. "I'm not sure. Is there something I can help you with?"

Should she show him the coin or should she come back later? Tattoo guy looked to be a part-timer, not a coin aficionado. "Do you know anything about coins?"

"A little."

She pulled it out of her purse. "I found this one and wondered if it was worth anything."

He held it up to the light then pulled out his jeweler's loupe to take a closer look. "Well I'll be darned. This is the second one of these I've seen in the shop this week. What you've got here is a Walking Liberty Half Dollar. An early one, too."

"Is it rare?"

He squinted through the magnifier. "As a matter of fact, it is. This one is marked with an *S*, which makes it worth more. The boss would have to grade it to figure out its value. Are you looking to sell it?"

"Maybe. You say you have another one here? Are they identical?"

"I'm not sure. Wait here a minute." He headed to a back room and came back with another coin in his hand. He examined it closely. "This one here is a 1920-S. Still rare, but not as early."

"I see." Deena was impressed with the guy's knowledge. She looked at the other coin. "Where did this one come from? Did someone bring it in this week?"

"I don't know, actually. I just noticed it on the boss's desk yesterday."

The shop door opened and a woman came in dragging two small children. The little boy ran over to a glass case filled with knives and started banging on it for no apparent reason other than the fact that he could.

The salesman frowned. "Look, if you want to make a deal on the coin, you probably need to come back tomorrow. Mr. Fisk took his car to the shop. I'm not sure how long he'll be gone."

She narrowed her eyes. "The repair shop or the body shop?"

"Clark's Body Shop." He looked over at the woman who seemed oblivious to her son's ruckus.

Deena left.

Surely, it couldn't be a coincidence that Fisk had a coin similar to the one someone put in her mailbox. But what about getting his car repaired? It was possible she had been wrong about Ronnie Clark. If Fisk had a wrecked black car in the body shop, the city might just be looking to replace its mayor.

* * *

ON THE WAY HOME, DEENA kept glancing back and forth at her mirrors. This wouldn't be the first time someone followed her, but this time she could be in real danger. If Fisk tried to run Billy off the road to keep from being identified, who said he wouldn't do the same to her?

She wanted to call Guttman. Would he even take her call? Would he agree with her that the coin had been left as a threat? What other explanation was there? One thought niggled at her. How could Fisk have been at the auction when it ended if he stole the coins, hit Leonard, and then ran into Billy?

Butterfly Gardens seemed less welcoming this time. Relief washed over her when she saw Gary pulling into the driveway. She really didn't want to go into the empty house all alone.

Oh dear. What was she going to tell Gary? If he got wind she was being threatened—even mildly—he'd be down at the police station faster than a roadrunner chasing a prairie dog. Not only that, he'd probably insist on her dropping the investigation. He might even drive her up to Tulsa to stay with his mother.

She shuddered at the idea, especially since she was so close to cracking the case and exposing Marty Fisk. *Politicians.* She should have known better than to trust the mayor.

Gary waited for her to get out of the car before opening the front door to the house.

"Are you okay?" he asked, leaning down to kiss her cheek.

"Why do you ask? Do I look that bad?" She pushed past him into the house.

"No, but you look like you're upset. Did you find something out about the case today?"

"As a matter of fact, I did. Billy—remember I told you about him—almost got killed today. Someone tried to run him off the road, and I have a sneaking suspicion of who did it."

"Who?"

"The honorable mayor, Marty Fisk, that's who."

"You're kidding. How do you know?"

"I dropped by the pawn shop to talk to him today. I wanted to assure him I was only trying to help with the case. Thought he would tell Guttman to let me back in."

"Sounds like you're playing with fire again."

"Whatever. Anyway, he wasn't there. He had taken his car to be fixed at Clark's Body Shop."

"I see. So you think he damaged his car trying to run Billy off the road."

"Maybe. At the very least, he scraped it when he hit Billy in the parking lot at the auction."

"But Fisk was at the auction when the police came. How could he be in two places at once?"

"I've been thinking about that." She sat down at the kitchen table and propped her feet up. "How far is it from the community center to the pawn shop?"

"Let's see. I'd say about three miles."

"Right. So he could have driven to the pawn shop, dumped the coins, and been back in less than ten minutes."

"I suppose."

"If only we knew if he drove a black car..."

"You mean a black car with damage consistent with the kind you would get from hitting a pedestrian."

Deena smiled at her husband. "You sound just like a cop."

"Speaking of cops, does Detective Guttman know about this theory?"

"Ugh." She told Gary about her run-in with Guttman and how he didn't want to hear anything else from her about the case. "The worst part is that I think he would accept my help if Fisk would give him the okay."

"Fat chance that will happen now. Maybe I can talk to Guttman."

"No way. I can't have my husband pleading my case. It's hard enough being a woman in this profession as it is."

Gary raised an eyebrow.

"I know. This isn't part of my job with Ian, but as soon as Sandra is back at the thrift shop, I'll be back investigating cases again."

Gary gave her a reassuring hug. "I've finally reconciled myself to let you follow your heart with this truth and justice stuff, but that doesn't make it any easier, you know. I wish there was something I could do to help."

"Actually, there is something." She flashed a bright smile.

"Uh-oh. I know that look. What is it now?"

"Nothing bad. Just a little midnight rendezvous with danger."

Chapter 18

DEENA OFTEN BURNED the midnight oil when she was a teacher and needed to finish her grades or complete reports. Gary, on the other hand, had a strict routine of being in bed by eleven o'clock sharp. Consequently, he was too tired to wait until midnight for their covert operation, so they left the house a few minutes after ten. Deena insisted they both wear all black. Gary reluctantly agreed but drew the line at rubbing charcoal on their faces.

They headed downtown to check out Clark's Body Shop. Deena wanted to look for a black car on the lot with damage to the driver's side from slamming into Billy. Perhaps the side mirror had come loose. If the car was there, she could then try to find out if it belonged to Fisk. If so, Guttman would have to consider it as evidence. Maybe then he would take her seriously and drop the charges against Wyatt.

"Turn off your lights," Deena said as they got close to the body shop. "We don't want anyone to see us."

"But I might hit something."

"Then pull over and park. We can walk from here."

She got out of the car and gently shut the door. She jumped and made a face when Gary slammed his door. Of course, he couldn't see her sneer at him in the dark.

The city needed to spring for a few more streetlights in this area.

Deena had never noticed the high chain-link fence around the body shop, but then, why would she?

They approached the gate and found it fastened shut with a padlock.

"Use your flash light to see if the car is parked out here," she whispered. "You go around that way, and I'll go this way."

Several wrecked cars lined the side of the building. Only one was black, a pickup truck. Plus, it had been rear-ended from what she could tell. Then she heard a scuttling noise and looked down to see a rat the size of an armadillo. Its beady eyes shone from the flashlight. She started to scream as it scurried away down the fence line.

"Any luck?"

She spun around to see Gary holding the flashlight under his chin like a kid on Halloween. "Stop that! You scared the be-jeebers out of me!"

"Sorry, hon." He switched off the light. "I didn't find any-thing on my side. I guess we should head on back home."

"Not yet." Deena looked over at the building with its four large garage doors. "We haven't checked inside yet."

"Forget about it. That would be illegal."

"Oh, come on now. Where's your sense of adventure? If you give me a boost, I can shine the light through one of those windows and take a peek. Then we're not entering or breaking."

"No, just trespassing. Don't you think the fence with the big 'Keep Out' signs all over it means anything?"

"Signs? It's a sign," she said with mock enthusiasm. "Let's go." She slipped the flashlight in the pocket of her jacket and reached up for the fence. Too bad she'd skipped so many exercise classes. She hiked her leg as high as possible.

Gary let out a huff but stood behind her and pushed. "If we get arrested, I'm going to tell the cops you blackmailed me or brainwashed me or something."

"Fine." She swung her leg up on top of the chain link and heard a rip. The crotch of her black sweatpants had given up hope of stretching. The sharp bits on the top of the fence scratched her leg.

This wasn't going to work. "Maybe we should go home and get a ladder," she said. "I'm coming down."

At least that's what she thought..

Her pants leg caught on the fence, holding her leg hiked up on the fence. As she tried to wriggle it free, the flashlight slipped out of her pocket and fell onto Gary's foot.

"Ouch," he yelled and jumped around.

A dog howled and then security lights came on. It felt like one of those scenes in a movie when the dark field lights up and the soldiers are surrounded by the enemy. She looked at the dog bounding toward them. Not the most ferocious of junk yard dogs, he panted and barked as though he wanted to play.

"Get down from there!" Gary said, starting to back away.

"Don't let go! My pants are caught. Push me up higher so I can reach my leg."

"That's as high as I can push you. Hurry up, my arms are about to give out."

She looked down. "Are you calling me fat?"

"Deena! Not now." He slowly lowered her to the ground.

She felt her pants pull down below her waist and her foot slip out of her sneaker. The rebellious shoe fell to the ground on the other side of the fence.

Just as Gary set her safely back onto the ground, she heard a sound that made her stomach churn. It was a siren. The cold November wind and the lack of pants made her shiver.

Gary reached up and gave her sweatpants a mighty tug, ripping them off the top of the fence.

She stepped on a rock, sending pain shooting up her leg as she hopped on one foot trying to pull on her pants. She had one leg in and one leg out when the squad car screamed up, beaming its headlights on them.

"Hands up!" said a robotic voice over the car's speaker. "Get down on the ground!"

As they lay face down in the dirt, she heard a familiar voice above her. "Mrs. Sharpe? Is that you?"

* * *

HUMILIATION COMES IN various forms, but none as awful as being caught in the dark with your pants down.

Apparently, Officer Hitchcock had no knowledge of a connection between Clark's Body Shop and the Dietz murder investigation. Otherwise, he'd have probably thrown Gary and Deena in the pokey. She made up some cockamamie story about how she and Gary were taking a stroll and, wanting to pet the dog, she got stuck trying to climb the fence.

He bought it. Hitchcock may have been the busiest cop on the force, but he certainly wasn't the brightest.

Gary was more shaken by the whole mess than Deena. He wasn't used to getting in scrapes with the law. If ever there was a straight arrow in this world, Gary Sharpe was the straightest. Luckily, after thirty-something years of marriage, Deena had managed to bend him just a little.

The clear light of morning on Thursday brought clarity. Deena needed a new plan to get a look at Fisk's car at the body shop. Obviously, she couldn't go herself since Ronnie Clark would recognize her as the crazy cookie lady.

She needed to send a man. She would never dream of asking Gary to go back there again. He was still suffering from PTSD — post-traumatic sleuthing disorder. Russell, on the other hand, would be able to handle the job expertly. She called him as soon as she got to the thrift store.

"You don't happen to need any work done on your cars, do you?" she asked her brother when he answered his phone. It was a random question, she knew.

"Why?"

"I need you to go to Clark's Body Shop and see if the killer's car is there."

"I'm having a hard time hearing you, sis. Did you say you are looking for a killer car?"

Deena often forgot about Russell's hearing loss from when he served in Vietnam. She spoke up and went on to explain her plan.

"I can go in and ask about getting work done on my truck. Maybe a new paint job. That should work, right?"

"Perfect. I knew I could count on you. If you can, take a picture of the damage and the license plate. I'm ready to wrap up this case."

"Will do. By the way, is Estelle there yet?"

The door opened and Estelle came in holding a bag from the doughnut shop.

"As a matter of fact, she just got here. Do you want to talk to her?"

"Nah, just tell her that I'll be hanging around the house today after all. Cliff is taking the day off to visit his son in San Antonio."

"Thanks. Why don't you come by after you go to the body shop? I'm anxious to know what you find out."

"Yes, chief. I'm on it."

Hurley ran out of the storeroom and yapped at Estelle. That dog could smell food from a mile away.

"Hey, buddy. Why are you here today?" Estelle pulled a corner off a glazed doughnut and gave it to him.

"I felt like having extra security — I mean company — today."

"Okay, spill the beans. Something is going on, right?"

Estelle and Deena had certainly grown closer over the past few days. That, at least, was one bonus of having her here. Deena pulled the coin out of her pocket. "You're right. This is what's going on."

Estelle listened wide-eyed as Deena told her how she'd found the coin in her mailbox and had gone to the pawn shop.

Estelle got much too much pleasure out of the story about the body shop and Deena's pants.

"Do you think the coin was a bribe to get you to back off the case?"

"A bribe? I hadn't considered that. I saw it more as a warning. I mean, it's not exactly like finding a horse's head in your bed, but it *does* make a statement."

"Are you going to the hospital to check on Billy today?"

"I'm planning on it. Maybe he saw Fisk or whoever was driving the car. I'm sure Guttman will question him after what I told him yesterday."

"Are you sure? Didn't you say Guttman thought Billy's wreck was just a coincidence?"

"Guttman may think Billy is just an accident-prone druggie, but he's a good cop. He'll want to find out if Billy knows anything." Deena sounded more confident than she felt.

Estelle brushed crumbs off her blouse. "By the way, who were you talking to when I came in? Gary?"

"No, Russell. He's going to drop by the body shop to look for the black car."

"Oh my. I hope he stays out of trouble. You know he can get a little nuts when he's nervous."

"Yes, but I also know he can be a smooth talker when he needs to be."

Estelle nodded.

"Maybe I should check on Billy before things go much farther. If he has a lead on the car's driver, we might need to go looking in another direction."

"You mean besides the four we've already followed?" Estelle counted them out. "Abby, Wyatt, Ronnie Clark, and now the mayor."

"Hey, Abby was all your idea, remember? You and your signs."

Estelle sucked in a deep breath and whispered, "I was just so certain I was right about those signs."

* * *

THE GAL AT THE NURSES' station gave Deena the number of Billy's room, so she headed down the long corridor to find him. Hopefully, he would be awake. At nine-thirty in the morning, the nurses usually came around to poke and prod at you.

Sure enough, Billy was awake. He looked startled when she poked her head around the open door.

"Want some company?" she asked.

He motioned with his head for her to come in. The room smelled of antiseptic, and the curtains were drawn. Billy's leg hovered above the bed in a cast held up by a pulley. Both arms were wrapped in bandages. He squirmed as if trying to find a comfortable position.

"Can I do anything for you? Fix your pillow?"

"Nah, but thanks. My chest feels like something's sitting on it. Hurts every time I take a breath."

She walked over to the window. "How about some light?"

"No thanks. It puts a glare on the TV."

"They say broken ribs can be awfully painful. Never had any myself."

"You're lucky." He glanced up at the muted TV. "Thanks for coming by to check on me yesterday. Abby and Leroy told me."

"You're welcome. Where's your mom?"

"She's at home," he said, diverting his eyes. "She hates hospitals. I can't blame her."

"Have the police been here to talk to you?"

"The nurse said that Detective Guttman came by last night when I was asleep. I kind of figure he'll be back today. Actually, I hope he does come back."

She hadn't expected to hear that. "Why?"

"I'm scared. Somebody tried to kill me. I want the police to figure out who did it." His eyes seemed dark and sad. "I've seen movies. Whenever someone is in the hospital, they're a sitting duck. I should have a guard outside the door."

Deena didn't want to say so, but from her experience, Billy might be right. He wasn't just being paranoid. "Billy, Abby may have told you that I'm trying to help you. It was my sister-in-law's coin collection that was stolen, you know, and her driver who was killed."

"Can you get me police protection? You are working with Guttman, right?"

Deena squirmed. "Well, not really. I'm conducting my own investigation, although I did tell Detective Guttman that I thought someone may have targeted you. I encouraged him to get your story. Also, I told him about the car hitting you the night of the auction." She bit her lip, hoping Billy wouldn't be upset with her.

"Good," he said. "That will save me the trouble. I'm pretty sure it was the same person—same car."

"So did you get a look at the driver this time?"

"Sort of." He glanced up at the TV.

"What do you mean?"

"I saw somebody, but it was weird. I'm not sure..."

Either he saw someone or not. What was he hiding? "Billy, were you stoned?"

He wriggled again and moaned. "Not stoned, just a little buzzed."

"Tell me what you remember. Anything is better than nothing."

He reached up and rubbed the cast as though trying to scratch his leg underneath it. "You're going to think I'm crazy, but every time I picture the driver, I see a dog."

"A dog? Like in the car?"

"No, like driving the car." He must have read the confusion on her face. "You know those big brown dogs with the long ears that they dress up like people and put in calendars?"

"You mean, Weimaraners?"

"I guess. That's what I keep picturing anyway."

This was priceless. Here she was trying to convince Guttman that Billy was a believable witness, and he's seeing dogs driving cars. Where was a hole she could crawl into?

Billy moaned again. "You don't believe me, I can tell."

"Oh, I believe you. That's the problem. It doesn't give us anything to go on."

"Should I lie to the cops and just say I didn't see the person?"

"No, you should never lie to the police. They are trying to help you."

He offered a weak smile. "Thanks for believing me."

"You're welcome." She stood up. "Is there anything I can get you before I go?"

"A hamburger and fries would be nice. They've got me eating mush."

"Follow the doctor's orders. Believe me, that's the fastest way to get better."

As she started to leave, she stopped and looked back. "By the way, what was the dog wearing? A shirt and tie? A dress?"

"A long brown wig."

Chapter 19

SEVERAL LARGE BOXES of donations had come into the shop. A woman in town who ran estate sales had brought in all the leftover items that didn't sell. These were the kinds of goodies Deena loved picking through.

She and Estelle rummaged through the boxes, sorting broken goods from things they could sell. Estelle, despite her privileged upbringing, had a good eye for seeing the value in simple objects.

"I can't believe no one wanted these dishes," she said. "There's not a chip on any of them."

"They were priced too high at the sale. Also, people at estate sales are often searching for antiques."

"Well, I bet they go quick here in the shop. In fact, maybe I should buy—"

"Don't even think about it," Deena said, taking the plate from her hand. "Russell would kill you if you brought any more dishes into the house. You have enough place servings to host the whole town already."

"You're right. It's just that mine are so formal — and expensive. Russell makes us eat on paper plates most of the time. These others are so cute."

The door jingled and Russell called to them from the front of the store.

"We're back here." Deena stood up and stretched her aching legs. Her right knee ached from the previous night's encounter with the fence. She hobbled to the front counter with Estelle on her tail. "What did you find out?"

Russell had that Cheshire Cat grin on his face he got whenever he knew a secret. When he and Deena were kids, it always gave him away.

"You were right. There is indeed a black car in the body shop with damage to the left side. It's a Toyota. Here, I got a picture." He held out his phone.

Estelle kissed his cheek. "Way to go, dear. I knew you could do it."

"By the way," he said. "I'm getting my truck repainted next week. They do amazing work there."

Estelle rolled her eyes.

Deena scrolled through the pictures. "Wow. You even got the license plate. Can you message these to me?"

He pushed the phone back toward her. "You do it. I'm not as good with all that technical stuff as you are."

Deena laughed and shook her head. "You can take apart an entire engine and put it back together, but you can't send me a picture from your phone."

Estelle leaned on the counter. "So what's our next move? Is it time to call Guttman?"

Deena hadn't really expected the car to be there. She wasn't sure what to do next. "After what happened yesterday —and last night — I don't want to talk to Guttman yet. He'll think it's another wild goose chase."

"Why?" Russell asked. "What happened last night?"

Estelle giggled then covered her mouth with her hand.

"Estelle can fill you in." Deena rubbed her knee. "I'd rather not have to tell it again."

"Okay, so then what?" he asked.

"I'm thinking about going to see Fisk. If I show him the coin, I can read his face. I'm good at that. Maybe I can tell if he looks guilty."

"What coin?" Russell looked at Estelle. "You're going to have to catch me up."

Estelle's face dropped as she looked at Deena. "You're not thinking of going to see him by yourself, are you? He could be dangerous. Look what happened to Leonard and Billy. At least take Russell with you."

"I'm a big girl. I know what I'm doing."

"Wait a gosh darn minute!" Russell said and stamped his foot. "The last I heard, you thought Ronnie Clark was guilty. Isn't that why you sent me to the body shop? What happened?"

"Oh, honey. That was yesterday." Estelle took hold of his arm. "This is Thursday. Now we think the mayor is guilty."

Deena turned as Hurley trotted out of the storeroom carrying something in his mouth.

"What is it, buddy?" Deena leaned down to retrieve the object. It was a wooden gavel. The kind a person would use during an official meeting. Like the mayor might use at the city council meeting.

Estelle gasped. "A gavel...it's another sign!"

* * *

OF ALL THE THINGS THAT Hurley could have dredged up from the storeroom, he found a gavel. Deena couldn't shake the image from her mind. Maybe Estelle had been right about this "sign" business. She didn't have time to think about it now. She needed to focus on Fisk.

The parking lot was more crowded than the day before. Pawn shops tended to get busier later in the month when money was short and people needed cash. That could also explain why business was down at the thrift shop. Of course, they hadn't kept it open more than a few hours the last few days. Deena had talked to Sandra about it, and she didn't seem to mind a bit. Then again, she was up to her eyeballs in dirty diapers and was operating on very little sleep.

Deena pulled into a spot behind the building and went in.

Fisk spotted her right away, abandoning his customer to walk over to her. "What are you doing here? I made it clear to Detective Guttman that I didn't want you snooping around anymore."

She resisted the urge to stick out her chin. "I'm not here as a snoop," she said in a measured tone. "I'm here as a customer. Well, sort of."

"What do you mean?"

Glancing around, she didn't see tattoo guy from the day before. An older man wearing a cowboy hat and a Steely Dan t-shirt appeared to be the only other person working.

She smiled. "I found something, and I wondered to myself, 'Now who has the expertise to identify it?' That's when I thought of you." *Yeah, you can catch more flies with honey.*

He threw out his hands. "What is it?"

Deena pulled the coin out of her purse and held it up, staring at his face. The look was obvious and instantaneous. He recognized the coin.

"Where did you get this?" His voice came from somewhere deep in the back of his throat.

As if you didn't know. "I found it."

"Found it where?"

"What does it matter?"

"Ricky, keep your eye on the place. I'll be in my office." He motioned for Deena to follow him.

She hesitated as a knot formed in her throat. She hadn't expected to be alone with Fisk. If she refused, it would look suspicious. If she agreed...

She followed slowly, like a dead man walking. Was this the point where he would take her out the back door at gunpoint and make her disappear? She felt in her purse for the pepper spray. *Keep calm. You've been in stickier situations than this before.*

Fisk picked up a stack of gun collector magazines and set them on the floor, motioning for Deena to take a seat. He sat behind his desk and pulled open the top drawer.

As he reached in, she held her breath and started to pull the pepper spray out of her purse.

He pulled out his hand. No gun. "Check this out." He handed her a coin. "Same coin as yours, just a different date."

She feigned surprise. "Huh. So these must not be that rare then."

"On the contrary. These are actually worth a pretty penny."

"Where'd you get yours?"

"It came in here the other day." He stared at the object in his hand, but his mind seemed a million miles away.

She waited for him to say something. The extended pause made her uncomfortable. Should she cough? Get up to leave?

Finally, he glanced back in her direction. "To be honest, I considered calling you about this coin. If I tell you something in confidence, will you not run out to Detective Guttman and shoot your mouth off about it?"

"I will. I mean, I won't. You can trust me."

He leaned forward in his chair. "I think this coin came from the Fitzhugh collection. The one stolen from the auction."

You could have knocked her over with a feather. Either Fisk was trying to deflect attention from himself, or he was confiding in her. Both possibilities were surprising. "What makes you think so?"

"I know those coins. I also know where this one came from. That's a concern."

"I guess I'm not quite understanding. Are you saying that you think whoever brought the coin in stole it from the auction?"

"I'm saying that there is a possibility of it."

She paused to consider what he had said. "Then why don't you want to tell Detective Guttman?"

"Because, the guy who brought it in is a friend of mine."

Uh-oh. She didn't like where this was going. "So why tell *me*?"

"We both know you're a sharp cookie. You might be able to figure this out better than Guttman. He tends to be a little quick on the draw when it comes to making arrests."

Again, with the sharp cookie. Deena wondered if anyone would use that same description for a man. "What do you want me to do? I'm not about to cover up a crime or break the law."

"What kind of fool do you take me for? I'm the mayor, you know. I just want you to find out how my buddy really got this coin. If it turns out he stole it, then he'll have to pay the piper for his stupidity. But if he's innocent, you'll be able to protect him from having his name smeared all over town by Detective Fast Fingers."

The whole conversation had thrown her for a loop. She had come there with the intention of exposing Fisk as the guilty party, but now he was taking her into his confidence and asking for her help.

She considered his proposition. It wouldn't be like she was keeping evidence out of the hands of the police since she couldn't be certain of the origin of the coins. Was this a trick?

Fisk's impatience got the best of him. "Well? Will you do it or not?"

"Okay. I'm in." Had she said those words out loud?

He took a drawstring bag out of the drawer and dropped in the coin. A stern look crept across his face. "Before we shake on this deal, I want you to tell me where you got your coin? For all I know, you could be the real thief here."

"You know better than that," she said. "I found it yesterday...in my mailbox."

Fisk pulled a handkerchief from his back pocket and wiped his forehead. "Sounds like someone was trying to get you to back off. I seriously hope it wasn't my friend. Did you show it to Guttman?"

"Not yet." Her eyes blinked nervously.

A sly grin came across his face. "Looks like I'm not the only one who doesn't trust that cop." He stuck out his hand. "You'll let me know what you find out before you tell Guttman. Deal?"

"Deal." She returned the handshake. "Now, for the million dollar question. Who brought in that coin?"

"A guy I know who also collects coins. He owns a couple of local businesses. His name is Ronnie Clark."

Deena couldn't believe her ears. It took a minute to find her voice. "I—I know Ronnie Clark. I talked to him the other day."

"Oh yeah? What did he say?"

"He seemed furious when it was suggested that he might have something to do with the stolen coins."

"Furious, like he was guilty or innocent?"

"Let's just say that he didn't take it well and stormed off. His wife blamed it on his drinking."

"Wait. Are we talking about the same Ronnie Clark? Lives over on Pine with his wife, Wanda?"

"That's the one."

"Ronnie Clark doesn't drink, at least he didn't used to. He's an avid hunter. I remember he used to say that's how he was able to get so good with a rifle. While all his huntin' buddies would get liquored up, he'd stay sober to keep his eye on the prize. He said they used to make fun of him."

"I'm just telling you what Wanda said."

"That explains a lot. Maybe that's why he…"

"What?" Deena couldn't take another dramatic pause. "You can't send me into the lion's den without all the facts."

"It's just that about six months ago, he started bringing me his guns. At first, he just wanted to pawn them. Then he started selling them. I thought he might be having money trouble, but he said he just needed to downsize his stash."

"Well, he downsized it all right. Wanda showed me their safe, and there was only one rifle inside."

"Huh. Now I see why he wanted to sell me that coin. He's obviously desperate for money."

"So he just brought a stolen coin in here to sell? Wouldn't he realize that you'd recognize it?"

Fisk shook his head. "It wasn't like that. He said he found it in his car and thought it was from the stolen group of coins but couldn't be sure. I think he was afraid of having it since it might be evidence from a crime."

"So why did he bring it to *you*?"

"I told him I would hang on to it for him. If everything got cleared up and the thief got caught, I would give him a fair price for it."

Deena's jaw dropped.

Fisk must have noticed. "Oh geez. That could make me an accessory or an accomplice or something, right?"

She looked down at the coin bag still resting in her hand and tossed it back on Fisk's desk like a hot potato. "I think I can check out his connection to the case without that."

He grabbed it from his desk. "I'll put it in my safe. In the meantime, you're my witness to all this."

Again, she wondered if Fisk was playing her. It just seemed too risky a move on Fisk's part to show her the coin and make up a story like this. For now, she would take him at his word.

"I'm going to see what I can find out," she said. "To be honest, it may end up that we need to tell everything to Guttman so that he can get a warrant to search Ronnie Clark's house."

"You may be right. Man, that would be a real shame. Ronnie's a decent guy."

"One last question," she said. "What kind of car do you drive?"

"Why does that matter?"

"Just wondering."

"I've got my truck out there today. I took my car to Ronnie's shop yesterday for some repairs."

"I see. And what color is your car?"

"Red."

Chapter 20

OBVIOUSLY, THE BLACK car in the body shop belonged to someone other than Marty Fisk, but who? It would be easy enough for Guttman to run the license plate and find out the owner. Deena would bet her bottom dollar — or in this case, her Walking Liberty Half Dollar — that it belonged to Ronnie Clark. Now all she needed to do was figure out what he had done with the rest of the coins in the collection.

Deena drove back to the thrift shop, her mind preoccupied with coins and cars and crashes. She walked in the front door and glanced around, expecting to see Hurley.

The door to the storeroom, which normally remained open during business hours, was closed.

"Estelle?" she called as she glanced around. "Hurley?"

The door opened and Estelle stuck her head out. "Oh, I thought you were a customer."

Hurley ran out and came up to Deena as though a freed prisoner. "What is it, boy? You hungry?"

Estelle twisted her fingers. "I thought you were going to be gone longer. I'll be working back here if you need me." She closed the door with an audible click of the lock.

That was odd. She seemed to be hiding something? Maybe she was planning a surprise for her birthday. But that was still two weeks away.

Hurley circled her feet.

"Let's take a walk and see what we see." She attached his leash and headed out the front door.

Hurley pulled her around the corner toward his favorite spot in the alley behind the store. An old Thunderbird was parked behind the building. She pulled on the back door. It opened.

There in the middle of the room huddled over a card table were Estelle and Penelope Burrows.

Estelle jumped up and let out a scream. "You scared me to death!"

Deena dragged Hurley in behind her. "What are you two doing this time?" As she got closer to the table, she saw for herself. "A Ouija board? Oh, heavens."

Penelope chuckled. "Deena, my dear, you should be thanking me. I'm trying to help you catch a killer."

Did Estelle really open up about the case to the biggest gossip this side of the Rio Grande? Deena played dumb. "I have no idea what you are talking about."

"Stop being so coy and come sit down," Penelope said.

Estelle nodded. "You really should hear what she has to say. It's quite extraordinary."

She had no intention of getting sucked into their game of Twenty Questions with a would-be apparition. Instead, she led Hurley straight past them into the shop and shut the storeroom door behind her.

It was just as well. At least Estelle would be out of her hair. She could use the time to plot out her next move. Questions swirled in her head. Where had Ronnie Clark been at the end of the auction? When did he leave? Was the black car she had seen him driving away from his house the same one that was sitting damaged inside his body shop?

She leaned down to straighten up the racks of shoes when the front door opened. Looking up, she saw her friend. "Sandra! What are you doing here?"

The new mother glowed as she walked in with the baby in a big pink carrier. "I've been going stir crazy and needed to get out of the house." She pulled back the blanket. Baby Sylvia breathed heavy as she slept.

"What an angel!"

Sandra gently picked her up, cradling the baby in her arms. "Isn't she a doll?"

Estelle came out of the storeroom. "Well, hey there. It's good to see you. Let me take a look at that precious baby."

Deena stepped back while Estelle cooed over Sylvia. After an ample amount of baby talk, she looked at Sandra. "Would you excuse us a minute? I need to ask Deena something."

Deena followed her to the corner by the storeroom. "Can you come back here? I think Penelope is on to something."

"Don't you just mean 'on something'—something like booze?" Deena watched as Sandra walked around the shop chatting to the baby.

Estelle whispered, "Just because she drinks a little doesn't mean she doesn't have insight into the spirit world. I had to tell her about the investigation. Since we couldn't finish our séance the other night, this was the best way to get to the bottom of things."

Deena didn't even try to hide her anger. "Ugh. You've stooped to the bottom, that's for sure."

"Penelope Burrows? What's going on back here?" Sandra stood gazing into the storeroom entrance.

Oh, great. How was Deena going to explain this?

"Is that a Ouija board? I haven't used one of those in years!" She hurried over to Deena and placed Sylvia in her arms. "Let's go ask it some questions," she said, heading to the back room.

Estelle shrugged her shoulders. "I'll fix this, I promise."

And just like that, Deena was standing in the middle of the shop holding her goddaughter while three crazy sorcerers conjured up spirits.

* * *

BEFORE LONG, BABY SYLVIA woke up and began crying as though she'd seen the devil. Sandra thought it best to take her home. Deena didn't try to stop her.

As soon as she left, Estelle came out of the back room. "Now, before you get your knickers in a wad, let me tell what we found out." She lowered her voice. "Marty Fisk is guilty."

Deena crossed her arms. "Is that so? And how do you know that?"

"We asked the Ouija board and it said 'yes.'"

"Well, that's interesting since I just left the pawn shop and found out for a fact that he is innocent."

Estelle's mouth dropped open. "But, I thought you went there to confront him?"

"I did. He explained everything."

Poor Estelle looked crestfallen. It wasn't really her fault that she was so easily duped into believing Penelope. After all, as the sheltered daughter of a rich family, Estelle probably hadn't been invited to sleepovers and never heard all the usual ghost stories. In fact, she probably never once had her bra frozen or her finger dipped in ice water while she slept.

"Look," Deena said. "I know you want to believe in signs. I know you want to believe that your mother is around and watching over you, but you've got to get real."

Penelope came around the corner. "Don't be such a naysayer, Deena. Believing in the impossible is what makes life wonderful. Now if we're all finished here, I'm going to get back on my little broom and fly away home." She winked at Estelle. "See you on Saturday."

Deena watched her flit out to her car, the Thunderbird parked in the alley. "What's happening on Saturday?" she asked Estelle.

"The police extended my community service for breaking into the shop. I'm helping out with the Bluebonnet Club's Thanksgiving service project."

"Oh, brother. That must be the same one Christy Ann asked me to help with. Looks like we'll all be together again."

"Sisters in arms," Estelle said with a sigh.

Deena groaned. "More like, sister in handcuffs."

Chapter 21

AS SHE DROVE Estelle home, Deena told her about the meeting with Fisk and her deadline to find out where Ronnie Clark's coin came from.

Estelle admitted the Ouija board method of inquiry was potentially flawed. "I tried not to push the little widget toward the answer I wanted, honestly."

"Don't you think if it could be used for finding real answers, then the police would use it?"

"I suppose you're right. I think it's like you said, I wanted to believe my mother's spirit was watching over me."

"That's understandable, but we need to focus on hard evidence. We need to learn more about Ronnie Clark's whereabouts at the time of Leonard's death."

"Russell is going to be furious with me. After the séance fiasco, he told me he didn't want me hanging around with Penelope Burrows anymore."

"You're a grown woman. You can hang out with whomever you want. But he's right about her witch tales. It's a bunch of hogwash."

Estelle stuck out her bottom lip. "Do we have to tell him about it?"

"That's up to you. I'd just as soon forget all about it, personally."

When they got to the house, Estelle invited her in for a cup of hot tea. Not wanting to leave on a sour note, Deena agreed.

Estelle headed straight for the kitchen.

As always, Estelle's house was immaculate. Abby must have been there to do her cleaning magic.

"I'm up here," Russell called from upstairs.

Deena climbed the grand staircase and wasn't out of breath when she got to the top this time. Maybe working at the thrift shop had done her some good. Too bad next week was Thanksgiving. They were driving up to Tulsa to see Gary's mother and sister. It was sure to be an all-out calorie fest.

She found Russell seated behind the desk in the study. "What are you doing?" she asked.

"Abby was here earlier. I was hiding out so I wouldn't have to try to make small talk with her." He turned the page of the magazine that lay on the desk in front of him.

"Is that the copy of *Country Homes* I got from Wanda Clark?"

"Yep, and you were right. Their den is amazing. I haven't seen so many stuffed animals since I stumbled on Estelle's collection of bunnies in the spare bedroom closet."

Deena crinkled her nose. "I know I'm a Texan and all, but I've never understood the point of hanging dead animals on the wall as trophies. It's just creepy the way their glass eyes look, as though they're calling out for help."

"You sound like Estelle."

"Why not just take a picture?"

"Sis, we're not going to get into this non-vegetarian argument again, are we? Do you want me to show you the statistics about the overpopulation of deer in this country?"

"Please don't." She studied the wedding portrait of Estelle's mother and father that hung on the far wall, moving from side to side to see if she could escape their somber stare.

Russell flipped the page. "I mean, I get it. The older I get the more of a catch-and-release kind of guy I am." He pushed aside the magazine and stood up. "All I know is that Ronnie Clark must have spent a fortune on taxidermy. You'd think he'd live in a mansion."

"Who should live in a mansion?" Estelle asked, carrying in a tea tray.

"Ronnie Clark." Russell took the tray and set it on the desk.

"He won't be moving into your neighborhood anytime soon," Deena said. "According to Marty Fisk, he's got big-time financial trouble. Looks like he's stuck in his brick ranch house on Pine. I wonder when those pictures were taken?"

Estelle picked up the magazine and read one of the captions. "It says, 'Wanda Bell and Ronnie Clark stand in front of their first trophy, a white-tail deer with a net score of 187, as they pose for their engagement picture.' Whatever that means."

"It's big," Russell said.

"Wait," she said. "Here's one that says it was taken in 2016. So it wasn't that long ago. Look hon, they have the same duck picture we have."

She handed the magazine to Russell and pointed.

"You're right. I wonder if theirs is covering a wall safe, too?"

Something tickled Deena's brain. "Did you say *wall safe*?" She grabbed the magazine from Russell.

"Yep." He pulled on the edge of a picture of ducks. It was on a hinge and had a metal safe behind it. "I ordered this one from the company because I liked the way the artist painted the drake's feathers."

"Feathers," Estelle scoffed. "Don't mention feathers to me ever again. I feel like such a fool."

"So they might have another safe…" Deena's eyes danced around the pictures in the article before locking in on the engagement picture. She read the caption again. Then it hit her. She sucked in a breath so hard she couldn't speak.

"Are you okay?" Estelle grabbed her arm.

She found her voice. "You're not an idiot. You were right! Pine, bell, feathers!"

"What are you talking about?"

Deena held out the magazine. "Ronnie Clark and Wanda Bell live on Pine Street and have a secret safe hidden behind duck feathers!"

Estelle swooned. Luckily, Russell caught her before she fell and hit her head on the desk.

* * *

DEENA HAD TO ADMIT she was a little lightheaded herself after the revelation that perhaps Estelle was right about the signs. Were they really there all along, or was she just trying to make something out of nothing? She shuddered at the idea of the ghost of Carolyn Fitzhugh lurking around the storeroom closet.

Still, she couldn't tell Detective Guttman about the possibility of a hidden safe at the Clarks' house until she was certain it existed. If Deena told him her hunch was based on signs from beyond the grave, he would never take her seriously as an investigator again.

She needed proof, and there was just one way to get it. She'd have to go back to the Clarks' house and see for herself.

"I'm going with you," Russell insisted when she told him her plan. He sat on the edge of the bed where he had carried Estelle after her "ordeal."

"Me too," Estelle said, trying to sit up.

"Absolutely not," Russell said. "You need to lie here and rest."

"Oh fiddle-faddle." She threw back the blanket. "I'm fine. I just had a little shock, is all. I don't know why I was so surprised. I knew all along that Mother was sending me messages."

She'd never hear the end of it now. Estelle would be buying tarot cards and taking up gypsy fortune-telling before long. Deena had mixed emotions. If indeed the duck picture covered a secret safe — one that Wanda Clark hadn't bothered to show them — then she'd have to admit the possibility that something other worldly could exist. But if she didn't find a safe, she'd have to figure out a different way to uncover Ronnie Clark's guilt.

"Let's all go," Deena said, looking at Russell. "We can tell Wanda that I brought you by to see her world-famous den. You can distract her while I check behind the painting for a safe."

"What about me?" Estelle said, slipping her feet back into her shoes.

"It may take a while, so be patient," Deena told Estelle before she got out of the car. "You remember how chatty Wanda was."

Russell fell in step behind her as they made their way to the front door. She rang the bell and waited. Part of her hoped no one was home so they could leave and she could come back later by herself.

When no one came to the door, Russell reached around her and rang it again. He leaned over and looked through the front window.

"What are you doing?" Deena asked. "The neighbors will think you're a peeping Tom and call the cops."

"Looks like the place is empty," he said. "That's even better."

He reached in his pocket for something. "Cover me while I pick open the lock."

"What? You don't really intend to break in, do you?" Before she could finish her question, he had the door open. "Russell!"

"Come on," he said and grabbed her arm. "This will just take a second. A quick peek at the den, and we'll be out of here."

It was too late to protest. They were already in the house with the door closed behind them. Deena felt like a cat burglar as they tiptoed through the front room. She nudged Russell to take a right. They were in the den.

Russell stopped, taking in the décor.

Deena headed straight to the duck painting. She pulled on it. Sure enough, there was the safe.

Could Russell break into it? No. She swatted the thought from her head. She spun around to make sure Russell wasn't thinking the same thing.

He was still eyeing the room in awe.

"Let's get out of here," Deena whispered. She waved her hand in front of his face to wake him from his man-cave hypnotic state.

He followed her back to the hall. She glanced around to make sure the way was clear. As she did, something caught her eye. There, sitting on the kitchen table, was a glass of milk and a plate of cookies. The glass was half empty. Someone must have left in a hurry. Or...

She shuddered. Maybe they weren't alone. Were they being watched?

It didn't take long to get the answer.

* * *

WANDA CLARK HELD A shotgun almost as big as she was. "I knew you wouldn't mind your own business. Why couldn't you have just stayed in your little suburbs and left well enough alone? Now what am I going to do?"

Russell held up his hands. "You're going to put down the gun and talk to us."

"Stay back!" She glared at them. "You have no idea what it's like to have money troubles. To watch your husband slip into the depths of depression."

"Now Wanda," Deena said, trying to control the trembling in her voice, "you don't want to make matters worse. Ronnie will have to own up to what he did. You can't keep protecting him."

"Protecting him from what?" Her puzzled look quickly changed. "Oh, I see what you think. You think Ronnie stole the coins and hit that man in the head. He had nothing to do with it. It was all me. Well, almost. I should have stuck to the plan, then we'd—"

So Wanda Clark had stolen the coins! Not Ronnie. That explained why he would have taken the coin he found to the pawn shop. He didn't suspect his wife was the culprit.

As Deena stared at Wanda, she saw her in a new light. With her long, drawn face and dark hair, she did indeed look like one of those big dogs Billy had mentioned.

Deena glanced back over her shoulder toward the window. If they could stall long enough, Estelle might get worried and call the police.

Or she might try to come to the door. They needed to keep Wanda talking.

"Look, whatever you did, I'm sure it was an accident or a momentary lapse of judgment. Let's just talk—"

"Shut up! You two sit down on the sofa while I think a minute." Using the barrel of the gun, she shooed them into the front room.

Russell took a quick glance at the window, too.

Deena wished she could read Russell's thoughts.

She had to think of something to say. "Billy. Billy Ratliff saw you when you tried to run him off the road. Even if you get rid of us, he's probably identifying you to Detective Guttman even as we speak."

Wanda's eyes, glazed and wild, widened. "I didn't realize you knew about him. Then I guess you also know that I'll do anything to protect my family." She raised the gun. "Anything."

"Then I guess you want to keep Ronnie out of it," Deena said.

"That should be easy since he didn't do anything."

"But he did."

"What do you mean?"

"He found one of the coins in your car. Your black Toyota that's at the body shop. He took it to the pawn shop. The police have it."

"You're bluffing."

"Am I? Call and ask him."

Wanda scoffed.

They must have all seen it at once. A figure appeared in the front window. It was Estelle.

Wanda turned the rifle toward the window.

Russell made his move. He leaped toward her and slammed down on the gun just as it went off.

The booming shot and crackling glass echoed around the room.

"Estelle!" Russell yelled as he jumped on top of Wanda. He wrenched the gun from her hands as Deena ran to the front door.

Estelle, ducked down behind the car, had her phone to her ear. She made a thumbs up sign, signaling she was okay.

"She's fine," Deena called back to Russell. "The police are on their way."

Russell, his face drawn and flushed, rolled Wanda onto her stomach. He held her hands tightly behind her back. "You're not the only one who will do whatever it takes to protect the people you love."

Chapter 22

DETECTIVE GUTTMAN was in the living room when Deena finished giving her statement. Two other officers stuffed Wanda Clark into a squad car.

"Where are Estelle and Russell?" Deena asked.

"They are still giving their statements in the back of the house."

She forced a grin. "Are you mad?"

"How could I be? You cracked the case."

"I got lucky."

He shook his head. "It was more than luck, I'm sure. Tell me, how did you figure it out?"

"Actually, I thought it was Ronnie Clark, not Wanda."

"She says he wasn't involved. I had an officer pick him up at the body shop just in case. I want to hear his side of the story."

"Wanda said something that made me think there was someone else involved. It may have been someone other than her husband."

"Really?" Guttman pulled out his notepad.

"It's all in my statement."

"Okay. I'll read it back at the office. Now tell me, why did you come to the Clarks' house today?"

"If I tell you, do you promise not to laugh or make fun of me or anything?"

"Hmm. I can't promise, but I'll try my best."

"Fair enough. It was actually Estelle who figured it out. Estelle and her mother."

"I see." He tilted his head. "Wait. I thought her mother was dead."

"She is."

Guttman twisted his face. "Explain."

She proceeded to tell him about the signs from the thrift store.

With each new clue, his face grew more serious. When she finished, he let out a deep breath. "I've heard of psychics helping with investigations, maybe this is sort of like that."

She couldn't believe it. She thought for sure he would give her a hard time. "Wow. This isn't the reaction I expected."

"In this line of work, you learn to follow the clues no matter where they come from. Were there any other signs?"

"Well, just one. But it turned out to be a dead end. It came from my dog."

"Animals are quite intuitive, you know. What was it?"

"A gavel."

"You mean like the kind an auctioneer uses?"

"Yeah, or the mayor. That's why I thought Fisk—"

An auctioneer? She hadn't considered of that. She pictured the auction house: Jeb, Leroy, the tin signs, the old truck out front.

"That's got to be it!"

"What are you saying?"

"It's what Wanda was talking about. She said she had a plan, and I think I know who was involved."

Guttman's face brightened. "I'm all ears."

* * *

AS THEY DROVE OVER to the Auction Barn, Deena filled Guttman in on as many details as possible about Fisk and Billy and the black car and Ronnie Clark and the coins and the warning she had received.

He seemed to drive faster with each new detail.

When they pulled up to the building, Deena noticed that the old paneled truck had been moved since she was there on Sunday with Estelle. If her hunch was correct, it was the same truck Christy Ann said a junk dealer had driven down their street the day Deena found the coin in her mailbox.

They found Jeb sitting in his office. The look on his face told the whole story. "I wondered how long it would take you to get here."

"How did you know we were coming?" Deena asked.

He pointed to an old radio. "I heard it on the police scanner. I figured she ratted me out."

Guttman coughed and shot her a look. It was a signal to let him take over. "So what's the story?"

Jeb leaned back in his chair. "I'm a sucker for a pretty woman. Always have been. When Wanda came to me for help, I just couldn't resist. After all, Ronnie and I have been friends for a long time. I didn't think it would be that big of a deal."

Deena resisted the urge to yell at him. How could he call stealing and killing "not a big deal"?

"You can wait in the getaway car," Russell said. "If something goes wrong, you can call the police."

Estelle frowned. "What do you mean, 'if something goes wrong'? What could go wrong?"

"It's always best to have backup," Deena said, not wanting an argument to slow her down. "Nothing will go wrong, but I'd feel better knowing you were in the car just in case."

She bought it.

As they drove into town, Estelle sat in the back seat ready to crouch down when they got to the house.

Deena wasn't thrilled with the plan. It was one thing to put herself in these situations, but now she had included her brother and Estelle. If they found Ronnie Clark at home and he got suspicious, this whole thing could go south very quickly.

Something crackled in the back seat, and Deena spun around to see what it was. Obviously, her nerves were raw.

Estelle was opening one of the boxes of cookies. "Sorry," she said when she saw the look on Deena's face. "I'm a stress eater. Want one?"

Deena shook her head. "We're almost there. Get ready."

Seeing the street sign on the corner of Birch and Pine sent chills down her back. She clutched the hunting magazine even tighter.

"Should we have called first to make sure someone would be home?" Estelle asked from her position on the back floorboard.

"Maybe," Deena said. "Let's hope the element of surprise works in our favor."

Russell parked on the street in front of the house. The blinds were open. It looked like someone was home.

"She told you her plan. Is that right?" Guttman scribbled in his notepad.

"All I was supposed to do was make sure the hammer price was low on the coin collection and that Ronnie would win. She planned for him to sell it so they could catch up on their bills."

"But something went wrong."

"Horribly. I didn't realize she was the one who had stolen it until Ronnie asked me for a ride home after the auction. He said Wanda had left early with a headache. That's when I put two and two together."

"You confronted her?"

"Sure. I called her on Sunday and told her I was going to turn her in. I was planning to. I should have. But that's when she offered me a cut." He hung his head.

Deena wanted to wring his neck. It's not like he wasn't going to make a fortune from the auction already. Greed had raised its ugly head again.

"I didn't take it," he said.

Sure you didn't. She waited for Guttman to jump down his throat.

"But you did do something, right?"

"Yes. I drove to Deena's house and put that coin in her mailbox."

"And what else?"

"Nothing else. Why? Did Wanda tell you I did something else? She's lying. I told her I wouldn't help her anymore."

"Did she admit to you that she killed Leonard Dietz?"

"She said it was an accident. She was running to her car and tripped on the curb. She dropped the case and the coins went flying. That Dietz fella got out of the car to help her. She got scared he would be able to identify her and knocked him on the head with the case. Poor guy."

"Jeb?" A squeaky voice startled them.

It was Patsy. She crossed her arms. "You cheating scoundrel. What did you do this time?"

Guttman pulled a set of handcuffs out of his coat pocket and slapped them on Jeb.

"Jeb Johnson. You are under arrest for conspiracy to commit a crime. You have the right to an attorney..."

As Guttman read Jeb his rights, Patsy continued to yell at him.

Deena shook her head. *And they thought Leroy was the black sheep of the family.*

Chapter 23

IT WAS SATURDAY and the clock was ticking. Christy Ann, Estelle, and Penelope would be there any minute and Deena still didn't even have one batch of edible cookies ready to go.

She got distracted with the first batch and forgot to take them out of the oven on time. The second batch tasted so awful, that Gary, her official taste tester, actually spit the bite out into the sink.

That's when she pulled out her reading glasses and saw that the recipe called for one teaspoon of baking soda, not one tablespoon. It probably wasn't supposed to be a heaping tablespoon either.

She peeked through the oven door and stared at the blobs of dough. Gary's mother had taught her to take the cookies out just before they looked done and give them plenty of time to cool. But time wasn't on her side. Luckily, she had bought canned icing and sprinkles. Toppings could make up for lots of baking shortcomings. At least that's what she hoped.

The doorbell rang. "Gary," she called into the den, "will you please get that?" She wasn't about to leave the kitchen and ruin her last batch.

Estelle and Russell came in. They each had a platter covered in foil.

"Set those on the table," Deena said. "Then you can come in here and help me."

Russell headed off to the den for an afternoon of college football and some guy time.

Estelle looked around. "Where are your finished cookies?"

"In the trash. These are my last, best hope."

"Oh my. Well, let me take a look."

"Why? It's not like you bake either. Didn't you have Abby make those cookies for you?"

Estelle faked annoyance. "I am not that bad around the kitchen. I used to hang out with the cook while Mother would go off to her social circles."

"My apologies, Rachael Ray."

"And by the way, Abby quit. Apparently, hanging out with Billy at the hospital made her want to study nursing. She will be starting a program at the community college in January and is getting the first ever 'Carolyn Fitzhugh Memorial Nursing Scholarship.'"

"Aww. That's super. I'm glad to hear it."

"Well, Russell was a little disappointed, but she promised to give me the recipe for her pork ribs. Let's take a look at these cookies. What are you making?"

"They are Polish sugar cookies. That's what the recipe called them anyway."

Estelle pulled open the oven door and peered in. "Are they supposed to look like that?"

"I don't know. It's my mother-in-law's recipe."

"Let me see what temperature you have the oven set on." She reached for the knob. "No wonder! You have the broiler on."

"What?" Deena put on an oven mitt and pulled the pan out. "Oh, good gravy! I must have done that when I turned off the oven after the last disaster."

The tops of the cookies were scorched while the bottoms were still gooey.

Deena threw the cookies in the garbage can, pan and all. "Now what?"

"Oh, pish posh. You can take one of my platters." Estelle pulled the pan out of the bin and put it in the sink.

"No way. That would be like stealing. But, I've got an idea." Deena pulled two of the boxes of cookies out of the pantry. They were the ones Gary had bought from Christy Ann. "Grab a knife and help me ice these."

Estelle rolled her eyes. "Speaking of stealing, did you hear about Wyatt Garrison?"

"No. What happened?"

"They dropped all the charges against him."

"I figured they would after they caught the real thief. It probably helped that you said you didn't want to press charges for him going through your stuff."

"It did. And what about Jeb Johnson? Do you think they'll actually charge him?"

"He's going to testify against Wanda," Deena said, scraping off a mound of sprinkles she had accidently dumped onto one of the cookies. "Knowing the Maycroft Police Department and the district attorney, they'll probably just sentence him to do a bunch of community service."

Christy Ann appeared in the kitchen. "I thought I'd never get away. The kids were throwing a fit and Parker was in a foul mood." She set a platter of perfectly decorated cookies onto the counter.

Deena tried to hide her annoyance. "We can take those for you if you'd rather stay home. I'm sure you can find something to craft or refinish or bake."

"No thanks. I need to go. Actually, I *have* to go."

"Why is that?"

She crossed her arms and pouted her lips. "I got assigned to perform community service for my little incident with Sarah Garrett."

So, she wasn't volunteering out of the goodness of her heart, Deena thought. *Classic Christy Ann.*

Penelope Burrows came up from behind and threw her arm across Christy Ann's shoulder. "Join the club."

"You got assigned community service too?" Deena asked.

"Yep. Apparently, you are not supposed to drink in a car even if you're not the driver. Such a dumb law."

"I guess I'm the only one here without a record," Deena said.

"You just jinxed yourself, my dear," Penelope said.

Deena pulled out a box of plastic wrap to cover the plate of cookies.

"Did you make those yourself?" Christy Ann asked, leaning in close to inspect the baked goods. "They look familiar."

"Don't ask," Estelle said. "She's had a busy week. Crime fighting isn't as easy as you think."

For a change, Christy Ann bit her tongue.

"We better get going," Penelope said. "George will be waiting for me. If I play my cards right, I might get a little action, if you know what I mean." She gave them a flirty wink.

Deena picked up her plate. "George who? And by the way, where are we going?"

"Didn't anyone tell you?" Penelope asked. "The Thanksgiving service project is at the VFW."

THE END

Works by Lisa B. Thomas

Maycroft Mysteries
Sharpe Image (Prequel Novella)
Sharpe Shooter
Sharpe Edge
Sharpe Mind
Sharpe Turn
Sharpe Point
Sharpe Cookie
Sharpe Note
Sharpe Wit
Sharpe Pain

Killer Shots Mysteries
Negative Exposure
Freeze Frame
Picture Imperfect
Ready to Snap

Beachside Books Magical Cozy Mysteries
(Co-written with Paula Lester)
Pasta, Pirates and Poison
Actors, Apples and Axes
Grits, Gamblers and Grudges
Candy, Carpenters and Candlesticks
Meatballs, Mistletoe and Murder
Honey, Hearts and Homicide

Visit lisabthomas.com for the most up-to-date book list.

Acknowledgements

THANKS TO ALL THE READERS who encourage me to keep writing. I feel your support every time I sit down to write.

A special thank you to my team: beta readers, Lia, Lindsey, and Tom; editor Kelsey Bryant, and cover designer Susan at coverkicks.com.

Most of all, love and thanks to my husband for making it possible.

Made in the USA
Las Vegas, NV
05 April 2024

88298352R00121